MINDED

A HAUNTED STORY

R L MERRILL

Minded: A Haunted Paranormal Story
By R.L. Merrill

Published By: Celie Bay Publications, LLC

Edited by: Kelli Collins, Edit Me This

Formatting by: Bob Houston eBook Formatting

Proofreading by: Marcy Cordova

Illustration by: Regan Kubecek

Cover Design by: Yosbe Design

To Kelli Collins

Connecting with you has been kismet. I needed guidance and experience. You've shared your wisdom and insight, and I finally feel as though I am growing as a writer. That means more to me than I can express.

MINDED: A HAUNTED STORY

When landing in Purgatory, no matter the cause of death, a soul must experience an awakening, establish awareness, and ultimately, achieve acceptance of inevitable circumstances.

For Maggie Stone, none of these options were ideal. She was a woman in control of her own destiny, not a pawn in some afterlife game! But in order to "move on," she'll have to accept help from an unlikely source dressed in black denim and pissed off at the world. Will she be able to complete her task, work her magic, and mind her kin still struggling with her death?

Louis Sheffield has spent an eternity in Purgatory for reasons beyond his control. When he's given an opportunity to earn his ticket out of his holding cell, he's irritated to learn he'll have to hold the hand of a pretentious, know-it-all, party girl whose every action grates on his last nerve.

But Maggie is not all she seems, and once he's exposed to her world, suddenly he's tempted to finally accept his destiny and embrace hope.

These two lost souls must work together against the clock to complete their seemingly impossible task. When their charges refuse to cooperate, Maggie and Louis must resort to unorthodox methods to create harmony from bitter chaos. In the end, it all comes down to choices and consequences they never imagined possible.

Revisit the crew from Haunted and find out if, once again, love can cure the haunted.

MINDED

to look after; take care of; tend
to mind one's kin

ONE

November 2013

"My name is Maggie and I'm a ghost. I guess. Damn, I sound like I'm at a twelve-step program."

"You are, my dear. More of a support group, really. Please continue."

Maggie looked around at the circle of folks in the dingy gymnasium and wished for a scalding-hot shower. The room was so dark outside of their circle of creaky metal chairs that she couldn't see whether they were surrounded by bleachers, windows, doors… Nothing. The scuffed wood floor with markings for basketball was the only indicator of what type of room this was. She wondered if she were to throw a coin out into the darkness, would it hit anything?

The others in the circle were dressed in a variety of ways, indicating what they had been doing before they ended up in the circle, Maggie supposed. Suits, coveralls, yoga pants. Eek. To be stuck in yoga pants for an eternity. Fashion faux pas to the max!

"What do you want me to say?" she exclaimed, irritated to the point of wanting to scratch her skin off. Some of the others fidgeted in their seats. They moved as though their asses were numb from sitting too long.

"Whatever comes to mind. You have been sent here because of your

D.D.S." The plump, grandmotherly woman in the pale-pink turtleneck sporting a steel-gray bun was quickly becoming the focus of Maggie's irritation.

"My orthodontist? Why the hell is he still after me? We paid him!"

"Death Denial Syndrome. It happens quite frequently, you know. Especially to stuck-up party girls such as yourself," a grumpy, heavily accented male voice said from behind a mop of black hair. He was sitting two spots over from Maggie so she hadn't quite noticed him until he spoke. She had no idea where she was. How did she end up here? Maggie was very confused.

"You lot come in here 'like, whatever! Gag me with a spoon!'"

Maggie attempted to turn in her chair, but only succeeded in swiveling her torso to face him. "Okay, Mr. Nineteen Eighties! I know I died. I'm not a complete moron." Whoever this guy was, he was oozing attitude from every pore of his denim-clad body. His bangs fell in his eyes, hiding half of his face, so Maggie couldn't tell if he had anything to back up all that attitude. But The Dead Kennedys, Minor Threat, and Fear patches, along with several other patches and buttons from late-'70s/early-'80s punk bands sewn onto the ratty denim vest, gave a little bit of a clue.

"Margaret, dear, what Louis is trying to say—"

"It's Bones," Mr. 1980s interrupted.

"Shut up! Your name is not Bones," Maggie said with a laugh and a flip of the hair. "That's so funny! I manage a band—"

"Managed. Emphasis on the 'ed'. You're dead, lady. You don't do shit anymore. That's why you're here."

Maggie frowned and crossed her ankles, the slight move all she could manage to complete. Her Louboutins were cutting into the back of her heels, as they had done forever, and her black party dress was constricting. It had been a long night, even before she'd ended up here. She wished she were naked in her own bed, cuddled up next to—

"So I'm dead. Fine. Whatever. Why am I here?"

Grandma smiled kindly and laced her fingers in her lap. "You are here, Margaret, because in order to exit from this existence, you must be prepared to purge your earthly ties and accept the choice you must make."

"Choice? Fine. I choose to leave here and get back to work. My boys need me."

Louis sighed, exasperated. "Lady, you need to get a clue. You're gone. Your 'boys' have moved on, and that's that."

Maggie pushed her blonde curls out of her face. "If you know so much, why are *you* here?"

Louis sat up from his slouch and ran his fingers through the black mop hanging in his eyes. Maggie gasped. Underneath that black hair was the face of an angel. Okay, not a real angel. More like a punk-rock, rebel-without-a-cause, bad-boy fallen angel. The complete opposite of her husband. *Thomas.*

"Where's Thomas? Where's my husband?" She tried to stand up, but felt as though she were weighted down. "Why can't I go? What is this place?"

"A holding cell? Purgatory? Whatever your theology calls it. It's a shite hole we can't leave until we've 'moved on.'"

"Thank you, Louis. Margaret, your death was tragic, and just as your life touched so many people, your death affected them profoundly as well. They are struggling without you."

"Then let me out of here so I can go back to work! God! What is wrong...why can't I move?" She was never prone to hysterics, but she was fixin' to beg like a dog at the table if it meant she could see her boys again.

"The power to move is all in your hands. You must accept the way things are and embrace your destiny."

Maggie was always up for a challenge. She didn't make it to the top of her game in the music industry by sitting back and taking it in the ass. She wasn't about to sit back and take it now.

"How about you let me go fix them up and I'll come right back? I'll do whatever I have to do then. I just need to make sure my Bones are doing well without me. Call it a leave of absence? A sabbatical? A fucking furlough or some shit?"

She heard a chuckle from Louis. "And what then? You'll see them and be like 'I can move on now'? Lady, you don't have a compliant bone in your body. You're used to getting whatever you want. No way you'll move on."

Maggie fumed and struggled against her invisible bindings. She looked to Grandma for help, giving her best *mea culpa* expression, hoping for some mercy.

Grandma seemed to ponder Maggie's request.

"Margaret, if you would like to stay after group, I'd be happy to discuss your options."

Maggie raised an eyebrow, not sure she liked the idea of being alone with this woman. She was getting eerie vibes. If Mage were here, he'd be able to say whether she had good intentions. Maggie couldn't read people as well as her friend.

Or if Devon were here...

That just hurt her heart to think about.

The rest of the session, which felt like it lasted an eternity, consisted of confession after confession from the other six or so people in the group mourning for their lost riches, bitching about how their kids didn't appreciate anything, or how they were too young, too healthy, or too important to die.

Maggie zoned out for a long while. It wasn't until she heard muttering coming from Louis's direction that she snapped out of it. He was looking up and muttering to himself.

"What do you expect me to do, huh? In Louisiana of all God-awful places? Sorry, Old Chap. Excuse the reference." He scratched at his chin and then stood.

"Louis, you know the rules." Grandma raised an eyebrow at him and he cursed under his breath before sauntering into the darkness with the sexiest damn walk Maggie had ever seen. And she'd seen a lot. Her years with Artist Management at Slade in Los Angeles had seen a constant parade of hot men. Louis moved like Jim Morrison, a sensual lope that accentuated his broad shoulders covered in faded and worn denim, narrow hips that filled out his low-slung black jeans. Long arms ended in graceful, tapered fingers. Slightly bowed legs finished off a near-perfect male specimen.

She'd always been drawn to his type, though she'd never indulged. Maggie had only had eyes for Thomas from the moment she'd met him

early in her internship. Blond. All-American smile. Successful businessman. Everything she thought she needed and wanted.

Fool.

"It's taken some time for you to become aware. Usually the deceased
drift into our group, have their awakening, and move on to their final
resting place."

Maggie perked up at Grandma's words. "Rest? I'm not ready to rest!
I've got so much to do! I'm too you— Oh. That's what you meant earlier.
Awakening. What is that? And how can I get some time to see my boys? I
miss my boys. How long has it been since I died?"

"Coming up on two years, dear."

The tears could not be held back. Maggie had held them back for so
long. Or had she? This was all so confusing.

"How long have I been here?" she cried.

Grandma tilted her head to the side and appraised Maggie. "Time is of
no consequence. You have as little or as much time as you need to come to
your acceptance." They kept talking about awakening, acceptance, awareness... Maggie was no closer to understanding what the fuck had
happened to her life.

"I remember the party. There was an accident, right? Can you at least
tell me what happened to Thomas?"

Grandma regarded her closely. "In most cases, we refrain from relating
the details of a person's demise. It isn't healthy. It doesn't heal the spirit.
It's important for the acceptance to occur, so the spirit may find its resting
place."

"And what does that mean? Heaven? Hell?" Maggie was willing to try
any approach to get some information from this woman.

Grandma smiled and shook her head slowly. "The resting place is
different for everyone. For some, it is a rest until their spirit is renewed. They
may revisit their time and place in a different guise or form. They may
endeavor to experience a new and different life. For some, however, there is
no rest. That is what this place is for. For the restless souls who cannot make
peace with their position. They cannot relinquish regrets and responsibili-
ties." She looked toward the direction in which Mr. Eighties had walked away.

"You sure like your alliteration, Grandma!" Maggie slapped a hand over her mouth. "I'm so sorry. I was brought up to be much more respectful."

Grandma laughed for the first time. "It's fine, dear. Those who stay here long enough refer to me by that name. I don't mind."

Maggie figured if she quit fighting her reality, perhaps she could make some headway. "I just want to see them and know they are okay. Not to interfere—"

"Actually, that's exactly what you would be expected to do." Grandma reached in her sweater and brought out a pocket watch. Maggie wondered, if time didn't matter here, then why would she—

"We operate on a different time here, Margaret. This watch is not what you think."

"You're just like Mage. You can tell what people are thinking," Maggie said, wonder in her voice. Grandma nodded.

"Margaret, let's simplify this scenario. Occasionally those with unfinished business are given a period of time to, well, mind their kin. Help them find their harmony. Clean up unfinished business. You must be willing to do your task and then let go, no matter what the outcome. Can you agree to those terms?"

Maggie was unsure how to answer. Her life had always been lived on *her* terms. She'd left her home in small-town Louisiana at eighteen to make her mark in Hollywood. She found great success, great friends, and what she'd thought was a great husband. Sure, things had been tough for a while, but she'd had hope that after the band's album release party, she'd be able to step back a bit and give Thomas what he wanted. A baby. Become his trophy wife. She would give up the glory for him, to make him happy. Surely then he would give up his jealousy. His anger.

"What's the catch? And what happens when I'm done?"

"The catch—if you want to call it a catch—is simply that when you have completed your journey, you must be willing to take the path that is chosen for you. Are you willing to trust in the process? Give up control?"

"What choice do I have? You know what my answer will be. I will do anything if it means my boys—" She choked back a sob. She would do anything for them. Devon, Mage, Star, Jade, and even Marcus.

Maggie's Bones. She'd watched them grow from pubescent boys who could barely play a note, to incredibly talented musicians with ambition and drive. Their recording career over the four years she'd managed them had reached heights they'd never dreamed of. Awards, hit songs, invites to play with the hardest-rocking metal bands in the world...

But she hadn't been able to shield them from the worst. Drugs, drink, and drama. That's what she'd led them into. She had been too proud to admit that they were horrifically over their heads in Hollywood.

Jesus, she was starting to alliterate like the old lady.

"You won't be alone in your task. You will be escorted by an entity who has had years of experience. Your escort will assuredly assist you in all affairs. He is quite skilled. He is waiting for you outside those doors. You will carry this with you," she said, leaning forward to hand Maggie the pocket watch.

Maggie turned it over in her hands, lovingly caressing the fleur-de-lis embossed on the top.

"The pocket watch is your talisman. It is not to tell time, but to remind you that you have a limited amount of time to complete your task. It will keep you grounded as you step back into a life you are no longer a part of. Time will not move as you are accustomed to. Never neglect your task: Mind your kin. Help them resurrect their harmony. When it's done, you will have a choice to make. Follow the path, or remain here."

Maggie jerked her head to look towards the blackness, only this time there was a set of double doors with an illuminated exit sign above. She turned back to ask Grandma what was happening. She was now alone in the circle.

Grandma had vanished, as had the invisible bonds that had held Maggie in place.

She stood shakily from her chair and sucked in a breath, smoothing down her dress. She wobbled on her three-inch heels as she moved towards the doors.

"At least I won't be alone in this," she muttered to herself. Her shoes clacked loudly on the gym floor. She clenched and unclenched her fists as she walked hesitantly towards the door. The metal handles were cold under her hands. She pushed gently, not surprised that nothing happened.

Her gym doors in high school were like that. You had to practically body slam the damn handle to get them open, which was often disastrous for the person on the other side waiting to get in.

The next time she pushed, she threw her meager weight into it. The door flew open and she stumbled out into the hall, stepping out of her heel.

"Not the most practical shoes in the world." The annoyed voice sounded from off to the left of the doorway.

Silhouetted by a single light shining in the hallway, leaning against a row of lockers, stood Louis.

Maggie's mouth went dry as she watched him slowly raise his hands to light a cigarette using a classic Zippo lighter. He cupped the flame in his hands then took a long drag, the red-hot tip of the cigarette flaring brightly in the shadows.

"Before we take things further, you should know a few important rules. You may not leave my presence or you will end up right back here. Argue with my instructions or put one patent-leather-covered toe out of line and I will send your arse right back here. When your time is up, no matter the outcome—"

"I know, I know. My ass will be sent right back here. Got it. Do you hate everyone, or am I just special?"

"Party Girl, I don't give a damn about you, or anyone else for that matter. I have a job to do, whether I like it or not, and I do what I'm told. End of story."

"But why are you here? If you—"

"Listen. I'm not here for you. None of this is about *you*. All you need to know is that I always get the job done and my charges get sent on. That's it. So don't try to get to know me, or ask me my story. It's none of your bloody business."

His voice dripped sarcasm and disgust in a way Maggie had never experienced before. Instead of being hurt, she was determined to find out just what the hell his problem was. He had no idea who he was dealing with. She'd dealt with dudes way tougher than him.

Always up for a challenge, Maggie was exhilarated by the idea of breaking down his punk-rock attitude and discovering what made him tick. She had to have something else to focus on rather than the gravity of her situation.

She knew she was dead, so they could take their D.D.S. and shove it. What she struggled with the most was the fact that she'd let her boys down. She never should have let things get so out of hand. The last night of her mortal life, she'd attended the band's record release party. Their third studio album was hot off the presses and though it didn't show as much growth as she'd hoped, she knew there were at least a few hits the rock charts were going to go crazy over.

Maggie had taken a short trip home on the sly to see her mama and arrived back a day before the party. That was in December of 2011. She had been confident everything would go smoothly. She knew her colleague and good friend Sherry Jordan had everything under control. Thomas threw a fit when she returned, but she'd expected that.

What she *hadn't* expected was that she'd arrive at the party to find her boys—her precious brother, cousins, and friends—in such awful states of intoxication. Mage had been so high on cocaine he was having paranoid hallucinations. He kept telling her she had to make it stop, begged her to go home and not be at the club. It took all of her managing ability to get him onstage that night. Star was so shitfaced he fell over a chair and cut his eyebrow so deep she thought they'd have to take him to the ER before they could even play. Thankfully someone had butterfly bandages or the show would have been delayed by several hours. Jade and Marcus were practically getting laid in a back booth. There were several girls crawling all over them, blowing them under the table and flashing their tits in the boys' faces.

Maggie had little tolerance for women who had no respect for themselves like that. But the kicker had been the shouting match she'd gotten into with Devon.

"I don't give a fuck, Richard! You screwed up the mix on the last three songs! I should have been there to approve it, goddamn it!" Devon rarely got confrontational, but that night he'd had more than a few hard drinks and even did some cocaine with Mage before getting into a huge brawl with Richard, their sound mixer.

When Maggie told him to calm down, he pulled away from her and screamed, "Fuck off, Maggie! You should have fucking taken care of this! Fuck you!" He stormed off to the bathroom and that was the last time she'd seen him.

Shortly after, Thomas grabbed her by the arm, still pissed about her trip, and told her they had to go back to the office because there were some papers he needed to sign. He dragged her out to the parking lot as she protested the whole way.

"Thomas! I have to be here," she pleaded, yanking her arm from his grasp. "Can't you see this is all falling apart?"

Maggie continued to argue with him as they climbed in the car and he revved the engine. She forgot all about her seatbelt.

"If you cared so much for your precious Bones, you wouldn't have left. Now do your job as my *wife*."

Maggie begged him to go back, worried there would be more trouble, but trouble for her was just beginning. She recalled reaching for his arm, pleading with him as he swerved, and then…

"What they say about dying being painless when it happens in a split second? It's bullshit. I remember," she said as she and Louis walked down the dark hallway, his tall, lanky frame beside her. "I remember feeling weightless just before the glass shattered. I swear I think I felt all of the bones breaking in my face. Then I flew through the air, hit the pole, and landed sprawled on the grass. I remember it now like I'm watching it happen in a movie. It was just like that horrific scene from *Grindhouse*, remember? With Kurt Russell? Stunt Man Mike? No? You don't—"

"No. And everybody feels their death. You're not the only one to feel pain, Party Girl."

"Jesus! Asshole much? I do have a name, you know. Actually, I have several. My family called me Maggie, my husband called me—"

"Pain in the arse? No? How about loudmouthed narcissist? Wake up, Party Girl. You're not unique. Everybody dies. Everybody feels pain. The only reason you're important right now is because you need to fix what you let unravel."

Maggie was unaffected by his name-calling. She'd had enough experience with people to understand projection, deflection…all those tions. She flicked her curls back over her shoulder and stuck her chin out.

"So what's the plan then, Sir Snottypants? Where are you from, anyway? You sound British, but there's—"

"Like I said before," he interrupted with a singsong voice. "None of your bloody business. We go where we're meant."

Unsatisfied with his answer, she grabbed his arm and attempted to pull him to a stop. She managed to slow him and barely avoided breaking a heel.

"Fine. No more personal questions. For now. How do we proceed when we get to where we're going? Will they be able to see me? Will I interact with them? How does this work?"

"Bloody hell, you ask a lot of questions. Look, just follow my lead. No one will see us or what we do unless it is necessary, and then it will just happen. You are not in charge anymore, you're no manager. You may have to use those skills, however. It sounds as though we are headed into a right catastrophe that's been brewing, and before you open that pretty mouth one more time, I'll not be answering any more questions. Are we clear?"

"Crystal," she said.

Moments later, the air around them grew heavy with a familiar scent. The hallway darkened until Maggie felt completely enclosed in blackness.

She followed the sounds of Louis's footsteps next to hers and prayed she didn't step wrong and sprain an ankle.

TWO

THE SCENT OF LEMON DISH SOAP TICKLED HER NOSE, MAKING HER FEEL clean. It reminded her of a brand new day dawning in the French Quarter, a place just as much a home to her as the city of Houma, or Hollywood even.

As the sky lightened and the sounds of horses chuffing filled her ears, Maggie stopped dead in her tracks.

"This is Jackson Square. We're in Jackson Square. Why are we in Jackson Square?" The gray skies dripped heavy mist until Maggie felt her curls start to tighten.

Louis gave an exaggerated sigh as he took in their surroundings with a sneer. "I take it this is your beloved New Orleans? Can't say I've had the displeasure of ever being in this cesspool."

Maggie rolled her eyes. "Do you ever have anything positive to contribute? Or is this what I should continue to expect?"

Louis's pink lips spread into a sly smile. His cheeks were mottled red from the cold. He flicked his hair out of his face for just a moment, giving Maggie a clear view of the sparkle in his gray eyes.

"Am I not a charming enough escort for you, Party Girl? Terribly sorry. I'll be sure to try *harder*."

He accentuated the word "harder," ending his sentence in a smirk, which made Maggie laugh. He had no idea that the more he tried to turn her off, the more he was endearing himself to her. She loved them snarky.

"Hmmm. So what's the deal? Do we get to eat and drink or are we just, like, wraiths or something?" She thought she was handling all of this very well for being newly "aware" of her ghost status. If she could have some beignets right now, she might just be able to get used to this afterlife gig.

"We can do whatever we want. People won't see us or hear us unless we want them to, and no one will remember us after we're gone unless it's part of our task that we make contact. Simple, really. Think you can keep up?"

"Think *you* can keep up with *me*, is what you should be asking yourself." Maggie rounded the square at a quick pace, heading up St. Peter and into the heart of the Quarter. Louis's boots kept up with the clack-clack of her heels on the pavement. Very few people were out and about, most were probably still in bed from carousing the night before. Something was drawing Maggie away from the center of the action towards, well, death. She turned left on Basin and soon found herself at the gates of St. Louis No. 1 cemetery. She broke into a fit of giggles.

"I imagine you are not the saint this place was named after." She turned to look back at her guide, who was gazing up at placards on the concrete pillars.

"You imagine correctly. Louis IX, the former king of France. He fed the poor outside his palace. Nice bloke."

Maggie dramatically brought her hand to her chest. Louis's expression went from contemplative to aggravated. "What?" he asked, most likely not wanting her to answer.

"Nothing. You just were positive. I thought my heart would stop. Oh just kidding. It already has!" She snorted and pushed past him to enter the cemetery. Inside were several families gathered around crypts. Maggie recognized a few people as she passed through.

"What day is it today?" she whispered.

"November first, I believe," Louis answered, sounding curious.

"It's All Saints'! Oh!" She took off toward the back and to the left, hurrying around corners and down pathways that were treacherous in her heels, but she felt that strange pull again. She stopped short ten yards or so away from the Dumas family crypt. She stepped behind the brick of another burial place to observe what was going on.

Two women were repainting the white plaster on the tomb and talking softly with each other. She heard familiar male voices that made her ghostly pulse jump.

"It's my boys!" It took all of her self-control to stay in her spot, hidden behind the stone. Louis leaned closer, his breath fanning her neck.

"They will only see you when it's time. They won't know you're here."

Maggie smiled through her unshed tears. "Yeah. They will."

"What's wrong?" Jaylene asked Sammara, her voice full of concern. Sammara's already pale skin went ghost white for a moment and she'd frozen mid-brushstroke. This morning Jaylene and Devon had joined Sammara, Mage and Mage's family to do some upkeep on the Dumas family crypt, and then later would drive to Houma with Marie, Devon's mother, to do the same for the Boudreaux family. The next day was All Souls' Day and they'd planned a feast at the Boudreaux family home.

"Just some serious activity," Sammara said in a low voice. Jaylene appreciated that Sammara felt comfortable talking about her "feelings." Since she'd become Mage's girlfriend, she said she felt as though she finally had people she could fly her freak flag around with pride. Sammara had shared with Jaylene that she sometimes picked up impressions in places where there was spiritual unrest, like an empath or medium.

Sammara carefully placed her paintbrush into the plastic cup she'd been using to hold her paint as the two women worked side by side. She set the cup down on the ground and stepped away from the tomb. "I felt a strong presence just moments ago. It's like we're being watched."

Jaylene watched Sammara curiously. She also took a break from painting the whitewash over the plaster and sat her cup down on a brick next to Sammara's to see what was going on.

"I feel someone familiar. Someone I know of, but have never met. Hey Mage?" Her lover joined her from the other side of the tomb.

"What is it, chère?" Mage encircled Sammara's waist with his arms and kissed the side of her neck.

"Do you feel it?" she whispered to him while staring across the way.

Jaylene gasped as Mage closed his eyes. A strong jolt shot through him and Sammara, visibly startling them both. Sammara turned in his arms and looked up at him.

"What are you—"

"Maggie," he murmured. "That feels like Maggie." Immediately tears filled his eyes and he let out a shaky breath. "Oh, babe. I miss you."

Sammara looked forward once more and covered his hands on her waist, giving them a squeeze. "Is that really her? She's not alone, though. There's someone with her."

MAGE COULD SMELL MAGGIE'S PERFUME. SHE ALWAYS SMELLED OF LILACS. He'd brought lilacs to her grave when they bloomed in the spring and he intended to do it every year. He missed his friend and manager. The second anniversary of her death was soon approaching. He'd finally found happiness with Sammara and was making a life with her here in his hometown. But all the pieces of his life were not back together. They never would be. Not only was Maggie gone, but now his band of brothers, Maggie's Bones, were on hiatus, with nothing in the works to reunite them.

Sure, he and D still made music. They played together in the Quarter frequently with other musicians who called New Orleans home. Star was around, but he'd had some setbacks this year and spent a lot of his time in Houma. Jade was doing his thing, trying to find himself.

No one had heard from Marcus since New Year's. Not personally, anyway. They still talked to Sherry, who was trying to keep their business interests under control.

He missed the chemistry, the magic that the five of them created when they played together. He knew in his heart, the way he sometimes just knew things, the Bones would play as a band again. He just couldn't yet see how to make it happen. Sammara encouraged him to have faith and let time heal their wounds, but it had been nearly two years since Maggie had died. The pain of losing her still resonated through him like an echo across an empty canyon.

Sammara turned in his arms and placed her hands on his face. "My love, I can feel your pain."

She always knew when he needed her touch. He closed his eyes and leaned into it, drinking in her healing energy, just as he'd done every day since she'd moved here with him. Once the band had cancelled their tour, he'd gotten busy with renovations at the St. Germaine, an historic building he and his band mates D, Jade and Star had purchased together and planned to turn into Club Haunt. He travelled with Sammara back to Hollywood one week each month so she could continue her job as Features Editor with *Feedback Magazine*, the most cutting-edge publication for hard rock and heavy metal, and now, with her guidance, the magazine was tackling social issues that affected the music industry and its fans. The club would hopefully be ready to open in time for Valentine's Day.

Just then Devon rounded the corner and took in the sight of them all staring off into the distance. "What's going on, chère?" he asked Jaylene.

Jaylene took his hand. "I think Sammara was having one of her feelings. She said she felt like she was being watched." She paused and then Mage heard her whisper, "I heard Mage say something about Maggie."

Devon frowned harshly. "Don't fuck with me, Mage." He usually did a good job of keeping it together in front of others these days, but Maggie was still a sore subject for him. He'd been especially vulnerable since his mother, Marie, had been diagnosed with breast cancer. She'd made it through treatment like a champ and was almost back to her old self. But after losing his daddy in a fishing boat accident, and then his sister in a terrible car accident, he was particularly protective of his mama. He'd come a long way from the devastating grief he'd held inside when they all first met Jaylene, thanks to her skills as a therapist, her infinite patience, and her love.

"D, bro. I'm not fucking around. She's here." Mage didn't look at Devon. He just kept looking in the same direction as Sammara.

"You and your freaky shit," Devon said with a clenched jaw. "What do you mean, she's here? Dammit, Mage, you know—"

"Devon?" Sammara asked. "Was she wearing pearls when she died?" Sammara seemed to be in a bit of a trance. "She's wearing a black dress and pearls."

Devon sucked in a breath and looked around. "Maggie," he whispered. Mage stepped away from his lady and put a hand on Devon's shoulder.

"I'm sorry, brother, but I think Sammara's right." He stood by his friend as he'd done for the past two years and gave him support. He believed Sammara. It had to be Maggie.

LOUIS OBSERVED THE SCENE BEFORE HIM WITH A SCOWL. MAGGIE GAZED AT the two men and two women Louis assumed were their girlfriends with her delicate hand pressed to her unbeating heart.

"How can she see me? How do they know I'm here, Louis?"

Louis swore under his breath and looked up to the sky. "Thanks for warning me we'd be dealing with sensitives."

Maggie turned to catch him. "That's the second time you've done that. Who are you talking to?"

Louis didn't like being caught. He had a love/hate relationship with the Old Chap Upstairs. He hated these missions, but he had no choice. Unless he accepted his destiny, he was going to be stuck doing this job forever. It was a battle of wits he was sorely losing. At some point he was going to get sick of watching others move on. Just not yet. It was as if he'd been waiting for something to happen.

Louis hadn't moved on, frankly, because he didn't give a damn about anything or anyone. He'd been barely hanging on when his girlfriend had handed him a fatal dose of heroin. Life had become so painful for him, physically and emotionally. He'd been living out of his car doing odd jobs and the like, often depending on the goodness of strangers. Then he'd finally gotten a break with his band and they were on their way to the big time in America. But he couldn't sleep; he had night terrors and was prone to anxiety, not to mention chronic pain from a childhood incident that nearly left him crippled. When he couldn't pour all of that angst into a performance onstage, he'd resorted to medicinal means to ease the pain.

He'd finally seen a doctor, once he got some money from the label that signed his band, and received prescriptions for pills in all the colors of the rainbow.

That was before he met Zoya. She'd found him at a particularly vulnerable time, and had everything he was looking for: a great body, a gorgeous face—and magic substances that not only made him feel good, but let him forget his misery for a while. He met her during their recording sessions at a hippie studio in the desert, and he'd quickly fallen in love with a dream of life with no pain. Instead, that dream ended his life.

His time in Purgatory had been one of rebellion. Screw women, screw caring about anyone but himself, and screw God for giving him such a fucked-up life. He'd known for a long time that they kept dicking with him to teach him some sort of lesson.

Well, bollocks is what he had to say about it. The only lesson he wanted to learn was how to make it all go away. Dying hadn't done it. What the fuck was it going to take?

"Hey," she said again, elbowing him in the gut.

"Ow. It's none of your bloody concern. It appears your friend and his lady are able to sense your presence. That will make our job more interesting."

"Interesting how? Can I actually talk to them?" She turned to approach them, but Louis's grip on her shoulder stopped her.

"Not yet. You have to see the whole picture first. We must observe them and see what is causing their discord."

"Ok, fine. But how will I know—"

THREE

Suddenly Maggie and Louis were swept away from the cemetery. Maggie felt as if she'd been hit by a wave in the ocean and pulled under, dragged to the bottom of the sea by the undertow. When they finally surfaced, they were in another darkened hallway. It appeared to be night-time, but Maggie couldn't be sure. A woman's laughter was the first sound she heard, followed by the pop of a champagne bottle.

She glanced around, trying to get her bearings.

"This is my condo. I lived here. Thomas!" She hurried toward the voices, leaving the darkened hallway and entering her dimly lit bedroom.

The sight before her gave her the urge to vomit, which would have been interesting.

"Do ghosts puke? Is it even possible?" She crossed her arms over her chest, one foot tapping on the floor.

The three persons on the bed were too busy, uh, getting busy to even notice.

"I guess you could look at it this way: It takes two women to take your place?"

Maggie couldn't tell if Louis was being his asshole self or if he'd just said the most hilarious thing ever. She couldn't even bring herself to be angry, the scene before her was that pathetic.

The   two   women   were   obviously   strippers/porn stars/groupies/wannabe actress hybrids. There was so much artificial matter on what used to be her bed, all she could do was gawk.

"Do men these days really prefer women to look like child brides? Come on, then! Pubic hair serves a purpose, people. And that one there? She looks as if someone sewed some rotten melons into her chest cavity. I'd be afraid she might break my nose with one of them, the way she's bouncing like so."

Maggie's jaw dropped. "Is that humor? Are you seriously making jokes?"

Louis's comments would have been wildly inappropriate in any other circumstances. Here Maggie was, watching her husband bang two incredibly hideous women in their bed, and he was giving commentary like this was a cricket match. Maggie let out a very unladylike snort.

"Oh, this is priceless," she said, gesturing towards the three contortionists on the bed. "He never was very good at giving head. No wonder he's got to have her do it for him. And damn, he's really let himself go! He used to hit the gym three or four times a week at least. That ass looks like it hasn't seen fitness equipment in a few years. God, was he always this atrocious?"

She looked to Louis for support and his lips quirked up. He smothered the smile before it had a chance to spread.

"I'm not quite sure whether I should comment further or not. Although, it appears they've made great strides in hair replacement therapy. You can barely tell that's not his real hair."

Maggie's eyes flared and she burst out laughing, bent over at the waist.

All action on the bed stopped.

"Whatthefuckwasthat?" Bimbo One asked. Bimbo Two had her mouth full at the moment and was quite oblivious.

Thomas looked around the room and rubbed at the back of his neck. Louis pressed his lips together to keep from laughing.

"They heard me," Maggie whispered. "Oh shit. This could be fun. Can we like, fuck with them?"

The deviltry in her smile defeated Louis' attempts to hold in his amusement. He gave a grand gesture. "By all means, milady."

Maggie squealed and picked up the champagne bottle and waited to see if they'd notice. They didn't. They were still looking around for the sound of her laughter. Except Bimbo Two. She took her job seriously.

Maggie shook up the bottle with her thumb over the opening and then sprayed the lovers with the sickeningly sweet liquid. All three sexual deviants screeched unbecomingly. Then she yanked the sheets off the bed, causing Bimbo One to topple onto the floor, smacking herself in the face with her horrible implants.

"Barbi! What the hell?" Thomas looked down at Bimbo One.

Maggie grabbed a towel and began flipping it over and over, rolling it into a long, tight wad. She pulled one end of the towel back and let it rip, snapping Thomas on his flabby ass hard enough to leave a bright red mark and to make him fall forward onto Bimbo Two. She cursed at him to get up, that he was squishing her.

"I don't feel so good," she slurred as they both sat up. She leaned over his lap and then promptly vomited all over Thomas's wilting member.

Maggie couldn't resist thwacking Thomas twice more, and a fourth for good measure. He attempted unsuccessfully to cover his puke-covered man parts, but she got in a good one that had him squealing in pain.

"Jesus, Tommy! I almost died! That's it. I'm Audi!" Bimbo One grabbed up her clothes and came shrieking toward where Maggie and Louis stood. Maggie saw out of the corner of her eye Louis nonchalantly stick out a boot-covered foot, tripping her so that she went airborne. She hit the slick hallway tile and went sliding several feet.

Maggie's laughter echoed off the walls of the room as the remaining two lovers scrambled to cover up. She approached Thomas, looking him over curiously, and then noticed the wedding photo of him and Bimbo Two on the bedside table. Where their photo used to be.

"How quickly after I was in the ground did you find someone to replace me? Well, I use the word 'replace' loosely. There's no replacement for me. You had no idea what you had. You wanted to control me and to take away my fire. When you couldn't... You killed me! You got me into that car and got behind the wheel when you shouldn't have been driving. And you're here living your life like none of it ever happened." Some of the wind had been knocked out of her sails by the reality before her. She was angry, hurt. "I hope you get a raging case of herpes all over your jiggly bits. It's a good thing I died before I saw what you really were."

LOUIS PLACED HIS HAND ON MAGGIE'S SHOULDER.

"Party Girl. It's time for us to move on. I think we've had enough fun with Tommy Sleazeball and his fuck buddies for one night. Shall we?" He held out his arm for her, feeling something he hadn't felt in a long time, if ever. Empathy.

If he'd been faced with Zoya in this scenario after his death, he wasn't sure he would have stopped at a few parlor tricks. He likely would have torched the place.

"God, I can't believe I was so stupid! Everyone warned me, but for the longest time I knew I had his full attention. I tried to be the perfect wife and then... I really do hope he gets that sad sack caught in a door or that his dick falls off from some awful disease."

"It's usually quite entertaining when someone catches their spouse in the act like that," Louis said. "But this time there was nothing amusing at all. That wasn't even a train-wreck porn shoot. That was just wreck."

They were now outside the building and walking down Sunset Boulevard. Louis was disgusted with the scene they'd just beheld. Maggie just seemed introspective.

"Wreck, indeed. I kind of thought he'd be a mess. I guess I thought I meant more to him. Strangely, I'm not even upset about him being with other women, if you want to call them that. Wait," Maggie said, grabbing Louis's arm to stop him. "I know they weren't the most, uh, attractive women ever, but what was your comment? About pubic hair?"

Louis felt his cheeks go red under her scrutiny. Maggie looked as though she was trying to stifle a laugh.

"Well, er, th-they were so skinny. A-an-an-and they were, eh, their, um..."

"Am I embarrassing you, Louis?"

Damn his stutter. "The name is Bones. Why do you insist on—"

"Because. It's difficult for me," Maggie admitted. "It still hurts."

Louis's whole demeanor changed. A little bit more of his snide tone was gone when he spoke. "The only person who called me Louis was my mother. She's been gone for a long time. I'm just not used to it."

"And you aren't used to discussing female genitalia in mixed company. I'll bet you were an only child or had only brothers."

Louis blanched. "How would you know that? What difference does it make?"

"Relax, Louis. I just like to get to know the people I work with."

"You mean like your husband?" He regretted the words before they were even out of his mouth.

Maggie turned on him with an ugly expression. "That was low, even for you. Look, I didn't sleep around, if that's what you were implying." He was mucking this all up.

"I was m-merely curious, Party Girl. Don't get your kn-knickers in a twist."

Louis walked away at a fast pace. Maggie trotted after him in her heels. "I'm not wearing any, for your information. Quit changing the subject."

Louis did not want to hear that lot. He was already having a hard time keeping his eyes from roaming. While Louis had assumed her to be a vapid, shallow, pretentious git, she was proving she was the exact opposite. The way she handled the bedroom scenario... The way she spoke about her family. Now, watching her curls bounce had him wanting to touch them. The way her perfect ass undulated beneath her short dress, and her shapely legs that tapered into the loveliest ankles... He was becoming obsessed with watching her every movement. The tantalizing thought that he could just slide his hand up her thigh...

"Wh-wh-what? Whatever subject are you referring to?"

"Female genitalia. Vaginas. Come on, Louis. What did you want to say about their vaagiiiiinaaaaas?"

This time she didn't hold back a giggle at his expression.

"Ar-are you always th-this vulgar?"

Maggie followed him as he practically ran up the steps and into a club. He walked right past the bouncer, who didn't even flinch when Louis's shoulder bumped into him.

ONCE INSIDE THE CLUB, THE MUSIC WAS SO LOUD MAGGIE KNEW HE'D COME in on purpose to avoid answering her questions. Fine. She could be patient. Besides, the more she pushed him, the more the poor man stuttered! How awful for him. Maggie really looked at Louis in his '80s, I-don't-give-a-fuck attire. He couldn't have been older than his mid-twenties when he died. She was becoming increasingly fascinated by him the more time they spent together.

And why *were* they put together, anyway? A musician and an artist manager? He called himself Bones, her boys were the Bones…

It was then she recognized the voice crooning from the stage.

She turned slowly to behold her cousin.

Marcus was singing, but it wasn't Bones material. Instead, it was something a bit sassier, more rock 'n' roll than metalcore. She leaned against the bar and sucked in a breath. Why the hell was Marcus here without the band?

She had a sinking feeling she'd just figured out why she had been sent back here. For some reason, her boys had fallen apart. It was up to her to find out what happened, and what, if anything, could be done about it.

"Man, he really shines up there." Her face hurt from smiling. She bobbed her head to the music, enjoying the almost pop vibe.

"That's your cousin? He's not terrible. Of course, he's no Jello Biafra, but my ears aren't bleeding as of yet."

Maggie turned to watch Louis kick back a glass of what was probably whisky. "That boy can sing anything. Metal, jazz, Cajun, R&B, Adult Contemporary even. He's got a real gift. Real presence."

"He looks like a right pansy," Louis said, pulling out his pack to light a smoke.

Maggie looked around and put her hand on top of his. "You can't smoke in here, you know."

Louis made direct eye contact with her for the first time. Their eyes held as they both realized she was touching him. After a moment, he jerked his hand back like he'd been burnt.

"I can do whatever the fuck I want, Party Girl." He deliberately lit the smoke, took in a huge drag and blew it right in her face. She braced herself for the coughing fit she'd usually have, but nothing happened. He smirked at her, his cigarette dangling from his lips. "See?"

"Whatever," she muttered, turning back around to watch Marcus finishing the set. He took a bow, gestured to the band backing him up, and waved as the packed house cheered wildly. She had to hand it to him, he sounded fantastic. He looked thin, a bit paler than she would like, but his persona was still a force to be reckoned with. She watched him walk off stage—into the arms of none other than Sherry Jordan, her dear friend and coworker.

"I'll be damned," she gasped, moving quickly toward them. She figured she'd put this whole unseen thing to the test.

She heard Louis curse behind her and felt him on her heels. She hurried across the club and stopped a few feet away from the couple, who were now making out.

Making out?

"Please tell me we can go home now," Sherry moaned into his mouth.

Marcus pulled back and kissed her forehead. Then he shivered. "Yeah, let's go. Something feels…"

He looked around with a frown on his face. He pulled Sherry closer to him, feeling safe in her arms like nowhere else since he'd been on his own. She'd really been his rock this past year.

His brothers had turned on him, but he couldn't bring himself to be angry anymore. That time had passed. Now he just felt empty, unless he was with the woman he loved.

"What is it, babe?" Her big brown eyes gazed up at him, worried. She took such good care of him. He would be forever grateful that she'd believed in him when the rest of the band thought the worst.

Being accused of sexually assaulting a woman at a club had seemed ludicrous at the time, but now? It was just the chickens coming home to roost. He'd been a player for so long, he'd forgotten how to just be himself. Sherry was the only one he felt totally comfortable with, and once she proved she'd stay by his side, he'd made peace with his fate.

Sometimes you aren't forgiven, aren't given a second, or third, or twentieth chance to prove your worth. He didn't blame his friends and family for their reactions to the accusation. He only blamed himself for not making changes sooner.

He took Sherry by the hand and led her out the back door of the club. She kept asking him if he was okay, but he was starting to feel that tightness in his lower back, which often meant he was too rundown or stressed out. His health was precarious and Sherry was always worried about him.

"HEY," SHE SAID WHEN THEY GOT TO HER CAR. "WHAT'S WRONG, BABY? AND don't tell me nothing, please? You seem so sad." Her hands came up to cup his face, forcing him to look at her.

"I don't know. I'm just...I miss them. I miss them all. I love these new tunes, but it's—"

"IT'S NOT THE SAME," SHE FINISHED FOR HIM. IT NEARLY KILLED SHERRY TO see this once proud, cocky-for-a-damn-good-reason man feeling so much pain. Literally. She could see the tightness around his eyes that meant he was hurting. She'd learned to recognize the signs after several ER visits and trips to the doctor over the past several months.

"Maybe you just need some rest," she said, pressing her face against his chest. After spending a year denying Marcus and pretending she wasn't involved with him, she relished his affection. She now had endless opportunities to have him however she wanted. He was usually up for anything.

It had taken her a long time to accept how she felt about him, and to realize that he really did love *her*. That she wasn't just a conquest. Since then, they'd been inseparable when she wasn't working and he wasn't in the studio working on his solo project.

He'd moved in with her after the fiasco at the mansion, which she still got angry about. How dare they turn him away after all he'd done to keep the band together? He'd explained to her time and time again that they were right to jump to conclusions about his relations with women, that he'd done too many wrongs to expect anything else. But thinking about it just got her hackles up. They were her friends, too, and she'd remained civil for business reasons, but she wanted to fly to Louisiana and slap the whole bunch of them for how much pain they were causing her lover.

Sherry felt Marcus breathe against her hair and his hands slid down and gripped her hips. He leaned down and kissed her neck, biting down just the way he knew would drive her crazy. She moaned at the sensation, linking her fingers behind his neck and tilting her head to give him more access. He trailed his lips, his teeth, and then his tongue down the sensitive column of her throat and over to her collarbone. Sherry could feel her tension slip away and wished desperately to have her hands on his skin.

"Let me get us home," she murmured, giving the back of his hair a tug the way he liked it. He grunted and yanked her pelvis against his, then he swiveled his hips to give her a taste of what he was feeling.

"I don't think I can make it home, chère," he breathed. His fingers slowly gathered up the material of her dress. "I can't wait."

Sherry gasped as he hooked his fingers over the strings holding a thin piece of lace in place. She'd never been so adventurous before, but Marcus made her feel so alive, so wanton, that she'd become much more accepting of his advances in what previously had seemed such scandalous places.

"Are you really trying to fuck me right here in this parking lot, Mr. Lambert? Is that what you think you're going to do?" It got him hot when she challenged him. Letting her fingers do a little walking proved that to her. His erection was so thick, and so eager to get to its happy place.

"Why, Mrs. Lambert, I do believe I *will* fuck you right here in this parking lot, just because I can't wait to be buried up here..." His fingers found her core and slid home with ease. She was so ready for him, excited by this little scenario he was cooking up.

"Mr. Lambert! But what if someone sees us?" She went for demure, but he always knew better. He spun her around so quickly, she barely caught herself with her hands on the hood of her brand new Mercedes, a gift from Marcus. She felt him rip the sides of her panties and quickly do away with them. Pity. She liked those ones.

"They'll see me making love to my incredibly hot wife." He slowly slid her dress up over her hips, causing her to arch her back. He fell to his knees behind her and began to worship her. Thoroughly. She only gave a slight thought to their surroundings as he pressed his lips against her.

Sherry wobbled on her heels, but didn't dare move. Marcus on a mission was an experience she'd never deny herself, especially when she knew he'd make her come like a tidal wave. He held her in place with his strong hands and licked and sucked until she thought she'd scream so loud she'd get them caught and arrested. Just when she thought she couldn't take any more, he did this thing where—

"Marcus! Oh, baby, you can't—" She let out a squeal just as Marcus stood and clapped a hand over her mouth. He chuckled in her ear as she panted through a 9.0 on the Richter scale of insane orgasms.

"Come on, chère. You can't get us caught now. I've still got more work to do," he whispered as he entered her, not quite gently. He was beyond that. Sherry held on for dear life as he thrust so hard against her, her feet lifted off the ground. He kept his hand over her mouth to keep her from screaming her ecstasy until all of Sunset Strip came running.

"You know when I get you home you're going to get more of this, don't you, wife? You know I'm going to be in you until you can't walk straight tomorrow. I wouldn't be doing my husbandly duty if I didn't keep you more than satisfied." He thrust even harder, until she stumbled, only his arms keeping her from face planting on the car.

"You won't be if you mangle my face, now get back to that husbandly duty— OH!" He hit that spectacular spot that always brought her right to orgasm. Every time. It was like his cock had some sort of homing beacon. Damn, was he good to her.

Marcus whispered that he didn't think he could stay in control any longer after he felt her core grip him tight…oh so tight. He came in a rush, holding her against him as he cried out the words that made her swoon. "I love you, my wife. Love of my life."

Marcus told her he still planned to have a ceremony in front of their friends and whatnot, but after everything they'd been through over the past year, he hadn't wanted Sherry to go another second without knowing how much he loved her, how much he owed her his life. They'd had a civil ceremony at the courthouse and made it official. He then took steps to make sure she'd always be taken care of, no matter what happened to him.

They stood together, panting and laughing for a few moments before the back door of the club opened and a large party spilled outside. They righted their clothes and kissed once more before Marcus opened the driver's door for Sherry and then let himself in on the passenger side.

"Seen enough yet?"

Louis's voice seemed to break through Maggie's paralysis. He couldn't believe they'd just watched her cousin make love to one of her best friends. On a car. In a parking lot. And it wasn't cheap sex.

"He loves her. I never…" She turned to Louis and grabbed the lapels of his denim vest. "He called her his wife! Did you hear that?"

Louis licked his lips and swallowed hard. "I heard something to that effect. I also heard a lot of, er—"

Maggie let out a laugh and threw her arms around his neck, pulling him in for a tight hug.

Louis froze, not knowing how to respond.

Something inside him cracked. It only hurt for a brief second before he felt something he barely recognized.

Longing.

Watching the two lovers had clued him in to that feeling. He longed for the kind of intimacy those two shared. He'd fought against it his whole life, knowing more pain followed where those types of feelings went. But as he looked down into Maggie's twinkling eyes, her joy spilled over into his empty shell of a heart. And he felt longing.

"I know, right? Damn. Well, I always taught my boys that they'd better take care of their ladies right. I'm so glad I destroyed their porn stash, or else that would have been—"

"Just like what we saw before. Thank you, no. I've had quite enough shagging for one evening." He pushed her away and turned his back on her, running his hands through his hair, trying to get himself under control. He'd wondered if *all* of his parts could still function.

He was painfully getting an answer to that question right at this very moment.

FOUR

THE LAST THING MAGGIE REMEMBERED WAS THAT UNDERTOW FEELING again, and then she found herself standing in the middle of a school hallway.

"No! No, God, please don't let me have failed! Please! Louis?"

"I'm right here, Party Girl. You haven't fucked up yet. This is the next place you are meant to see."

She whirled around to see Louis lighting another cigarette. "I think it's too late to kill yourself with cancer," she joked.

Louis went stone-faced and froze with his cigarette between his fingers. "For your information, I did not do myself in. It was not a suicide. I certainly didn't plan on ending up dead, did you? Are you really that stupid? Was that too many sentences for you? I'll try to dumb it down a little for you next time." He turned away from her and stomped off toward double doors and sunlight.

Maggie knew she'd hit a sore spot as soon as the words left her mouth. It all made sense now. She had a vague memory of someone telling her once that people who committed suicide were sentenced to become civil servants in the afterlife. Or was that *Beetlejuice*? Anyway, it was a rotten thing to say.

Apparently they weren't on close enough terms for her to get away with her usual sense of humor. She'd pissed off enough men in her life to know when to give one his space, and that's exactly what she intended to do. That, and see what the hell she was doing in a school hallway.

She wandered a bit farther down the hall, looking through windows into lecture auditoriums. Some were filled with eager co-eds. Some were half empty. One held a familiar, beloved face. She opened the door and her un-breath caught in her dead chest.

Upon first glance, he would stand out as the most beautiful man on campus. He'd appear so perfectly formed, a person would think he was a model for sure. He sat near the middle of the stadium seating, alone in the lecture hall. He had in earbuds and appeared to be studying. His leg bounced in time to music only he could hear.

Maggie couldn't help herself. She approached him and slid into the seat next to him so she could peer over his shoulder. She clapped a hand over her mouth when she discovered what he was doing.

Jade Michel Lambert—prettiest damn guitar player to ever come off the Sunset Strip, the goofiest kid she'd known, the lady killer so many women had sought to bed...her little cousin—was doing Statistics. And slaying it.

She watched him work problem after problem confidently. She remembered enough from her time at UCLA to know he was doing it right! Fascinated, she peeked into his satchel and found textbooks for Comic Literature, World Civilizations I, and Economics.

"I'm so proud of you," she whispered.

Jade dropped his pencil onto the desk at the sound of her voice and looked around with a frown. Then he picked it up and went right back to work.

Maggie noticed that the classroom was filling up quickly and the professor was beginning to write notes on the board. Jade closed up his math work and tucked it into his satchel. It was then Maggie realized he'd cut off his hair. Once down to his waist, it was now cut stylishly to fall in layers around his jawline. He looked sophisticated in a sweater and jeans with a scarf and untied work boots.

The only giveaways that he was a rock star in disguise were the tattoos peeking out from under his sleeves and the wide gauges in his ears. They were mostly hidden in his shiny black hair, but when he shook his hair out of his face, they appeared.

As the professor started to speak, Jade's lips split into a huge smile. It was as though he was excited to be discussing a novel by Tom Robbins. Maggie was so proud when he engaged the professor in a good-natured debate about the meaning of one passage.

The door opened below and she caught sight of Louis just as the pocket watch grew warm hidden in the hem of her dress. Before Louis could tell her no, Maggie reached over and took the pen off of Jade's desk and scribbled a note to him on his paper. He never noticed.

When she stood, she automatically reached out and squeezed his shoulder, something she'd always done to her boys when she checked on them, whether they were doing homework at a table at her mama's restaurant, or playing really well in a practice studio. She'd watched Jade grow up, but somehow missed him turning into a man.

Tears filled her eyes as she started to move her hand.

But Jade must have felt her. He reached up to rub at his shoulder, as though he felt something on him. His hand brushed hers.

Maggie felt a zap, as though electricity had shot through her body. Jade jumped, knocking his notebook and novel to the floor with a loud thwack.

"Mr. Lambert? Everything alright up there?" The professor seemed fairly amused and a few people in the class laughed once they noticed Jade's expression. His eyes were wide and full of wonder.

"Yeah, yeah. Sorry, Professor Laughton." He got himself under control, but Maggie could see as she backed away that his hands were shaking and he kept glancing in her direction. He rubbed at his neck one last time before she reached the door.

Then he noticed her note.

"What in the bloody hell was that?" Louis asked as he yanked her by the arm out the door. It slammed shut, the noise causing a few shrieks from inside the classroom.

"He's doing it! He's always been so smart, but he never believed in himself. Goddammit, he's doing it! I love that kid," she said, wiping tears from her eyes. Happy tears. She hadn't felt the pervasive sadness emanating from Jade that she had from the others. Perhaps he really was finding himself. She hoped he found what he was looking for.

Louis backed Maggie up against a glass display case. "What the fuck did you think you were doing, writing on his paper? You broke a major rule, Party Girl. Leave no trace. Nothing indisputable. What did you write?"

Everything went dark as Maggie was pulled under once again.

"JADE? BUDDY, WHAT'S UP?"

Jade was really glad to talk to his best friend. Mage was so damn proud of him for going to school. When Jaylene mentioned it last year during a rousing game of Trivial Pursuit, Jade was excited by the idea. But being in a band meant no life *but* the band.

When things fell apart in L.A. last December because of Marcus's indiscretions, the five brothers in arms had basically scattered in the wind. Not seeing Mage every day took a long time to get used to. They'd been the closest friends within the band, had been ever since Jade found Mage in middle school. Thankfully, Jade loved Sammara almost as much as Mage did, and the three of them had spent some quality time together whenever Jade's school schedule and Sammara and Mage's travel schedule allowed. It never felt like an odd-man-out situation. But school was really fulfilling him in a way the band never did. He was always just the rhythm guitar player and Marcus's little brother, or Devon's cousin. Now he was developing his own path, and Mage always seemed to want the best for him.

"I need to see you guys. All of you guys. Christmas is next week. Can we, please? Something really weird happened to me today and I need to see you."

Mage paused. "I agree. Mrs. Marie asked us to all come out to the Houma house for Christmas Eve. She wants us together, and after the year she's had, I'm inclined to do whatever she asks, including bringing her the damn Eiffel Tower if that makes her happy."

Jade chuckled. "It really would be nice. So you and Sammara, Devon and Jaylene? Star and Mackenzie? How about Marcus?"

He missed his brother, but he hadn't spoken to him since the day Marcus walked out of the mansion, slamming the door behind him.

That had really been the last straw for Jade. He'd stood by Marcus through all of his asshole moments because he'd believed in him. But after he'd first made such awful comments to Jaylene, about her thinking she could control Devon because she was fucking him, and then went on and on about the girl who accused him of rape? In front of Sammara, who'd recently joined their family and was recovering from a similar horrible experience? There was no damn excuse for that behavior. As hard as it was to let him go, Jade wasn't willing to sit back and keep his mouth shut any longer. He was tired of the drama, and Marcus seemed to be at the root of all of it.

"The girls are trying to get ahold of Sherry. It's been awhile since they've heard from her. Speaking of which, have you heard from Star? Has he been at Mackenzie's?"

When Jade, Mage, Star and Devon returned to New Orleans after the fiasco at the mansion, Jade hadn't been really sure where the hell he was going to end up. Then Devon and Jaylene moved in with his aunt Marie, and Jaylene asked Jade to stay at her place to keep an eye on things—and Mackenzie.

Star and his girl living together turned out to be drama of the highest order. Star spent almost as many nights crashing with Jade as he did with Mackenzie. He wasn't handling the free time well. Drumming had been the only thing he could count on in life, and without it, he was kind of lost.

"Bro, I haven't seen him in about a month. Last I heard, he was staying with his uncle in Houma. I'll try to find him and get him over there." Jade sighed. His heart hurt. He missed his family and friends, even his dirtbag brother.

"It's important we be together that night. I just…"

"Say no more," Jade said. He knew if Mage was saying it, something was up. "I feel you. I'll be there." They talked logistics about getting out to Houma. If the weather wasn't bad, he might just ride his motorcycle.

Living in the French Quarter made having a car difficult. A bike was perfect, as long as it wasn't storming.

Jade hung up and touched his shoulder again. It still felt warm from earlier. He'd felt something. Something he desperately needed to feel again. He knew if anyone could fix this mess they were in, it would be his cousin, their manager. Losing her had been the beginning of the end of the band, and now her absence stung that much worse.

The words on his paper in class, not in his handwriting, bolstered his belief that something bigger than all of them was happening.

FIVE

Maggie and Louis had been walking in the dark for what felt like weeks, and may well have been. All she saw around her was blackness. She only knew Louis was there because he was chain smoking like a fiend.

"I was out of line earlier, whenever that was," she finally said, hoping for some sort of connection. Anything to break up the void. "That joke. About cancer. For all I know, that's what could have..." How did one broach the subject of someone's demise in a politically correct way? Maggie was desperate to hear his voice, hear something. She felt the anguish and anxiety pressing in on her from all sides. She felt lost.

"I didn't die of cancer, Party Girl. If that's what's got you all melancholy over there, you can relax."

She focused on the sound of his boots pounding the pavement next to her and his intake of breath with every drag he took on his cigarette. It wasn't much, but it was comforting. As long as she heard him moving, she knew she wasn't lost. Permanently.

"Never in all the years I've been sentenced to this job have I ever had such peculiar situations. It's like you are so tied into them that they can feel you, even in death. How does that happen? What's so damn special about you that all of these people can't let you go? It's like your life force refuses to be silent. You've been out of their lives for almost two fucking years, and yet they could still smell you. Feel you. Even on my own journey to acceptance, or whatever the fuck you want to call it, no one saw me. No one felt me. All I saw was life going on without me. 'Bones? Yeah, a shame, that. He had the perfect voice, so much talent. Well, then. Who's next?' They didn't even have a fucking funeral or memorial service! Just left my body out in the desert for the scavengers to pick at."

He stopped walking and stomped his foot. "And why the fuck am I telling you this?"

Maggie hung on every word that came from Louis. She knew his death had to be awful. But this? "Tell me what happened." She could hear his breath going in and out heavily from his chest. She felt him brush against her as he shifted his position.

"Whatever would I want to do that for?"

"Because! Dammit, Louis! I want to know. If I'm supposed to trust you and do what you say, I deserve to know what happened, why you haven't 'moved on.' Tell me."

Maggie heard him growl and then his hands grasped the sides of her head, hard.

"Alright, then. I'll bloody show you."

Maggie felt pain throughout her entire body, as if she'd been shot out of a rocket and she was on fire. All the air sucked out of her lungs, making her screams noiseless. Images flashed around her at high speeds until she saw a sign crudely carved into wood in all lowercase letters: desert rose oasis.

She slammed into an invisible wall just outside a door. Trying to figure out what the hell was happening, she looked down at herself—and saw a familiar pair of black jeans and a faded blue denim vest.

The room before her was full of people dancing and taking hits off a giant hookah. Musicians played loudly in a corner. Someone handed her a beer and she waved it off, knowing she needed something heavier than that to get her through the pain. Every step shot shards of glass through her kneecaps and up her thighs. Her tailbone throbbed and every breath hurt her ribs.

A gorgeous woman with long dark brown hair appeared in front of her, smiling and coaxing her forward. She was topless, her tresses covering her small breasts, and low-slung corduroy bellbottoms fit her tightly across the ass.

"You have time before you play. Come play with me first, Bones."

Maggie realized she was about to experience Louis's death. Her still heart pounded as though she was about to have a panic attack, but she focused on that smile and the curve of those hips leading her out the back of the house and toward a trailer. Climbing the two steps was so painful, she almost cried out, and then the woman's hands were pulling her in the door.

"Zoya," she heard Louis's voice say, almost in a worshipful tone. The woman unzipped her pants and stepped out of them gracefully. She had a belly chain on, and from the center of the chain hung a small vial, low enough it brushed her pubic hair when she moved.

"Is that for me?" Maggie heard Louis ask. The woman lifted her hair up and raised her hands above her head, letting it fall around her as she swayed to the music still audible from the house.

"It might be. You have to show me how bad you want it first, baby." She lay back on the bed and spread her legs. Maggie could feel lust coming from Louis, but it was overshadowed by something closer to distress. Agony ripped through her borrowed body as she approached the bed and gingerly dropped to her knees. She wanted to beg for something, anything to make the pain go away, but was too proud to do so.

Maggie had never been so close to another woman's core before, and had no idea what was about to happen. The images blurred for a few moments and then she watched as Zoya poured powder from the vial onto her flat stomach and encouraged Louis to take what he really wanted.

Her head was swimming with so many feelings, but first and foremost was despair. How had he come to this? Why must he live his life on his knees, begging for relief from his pain? He was so tired. Maggie could feel it all and wanted to cry out from the injustice, but then insistent hands pulled her face closer to the powder.

The next images were like flashes from a camera

—worried faces, swearing voices.

"What the fuck am I supposed to do with him? He's dying!"

"If we take him into town—"

"Fuck that, Zoya. You're just going to have to live with his death. I *told* you that shit wasn't ready yet! It was too fucking strong. Get some of the others to help you carry him out past the sacred circle. Perhaps he'll find his peace under the desert sky."

Male voices laughed while Zoya continued to shriek and freak out.

Hands lifted her borrowed body from the floor and banged her around as they exited the trailer. Everything hurt, she felt as if she needed to vomit, and her head was so fuzzy it sounded as though it was stuck in a beehive. She tried to make a sound to let them know she was alive, but no one paid any attention. They joked as they bounced her along a dirt path away from the house. They passed a bonfire with naked people dancing and fucking in the light from the flames and kept on going.

She hit the ground hard and then felt hands going through her pockets. She moaned, but heard Louis's voice. A foot nudged at her midsection. "He'll be dead in a very short time. The desert will take care of him."

Footsteps moved away from her and she was utterly alone under the most beautiful sky she'd ever seen. The pain was unbearable, but she could no longer move. The last thing she recalled was seeing a shooting star before everything went black. And the pain was gone.

Maggie pushed away from Louis and screamed. She ran her hands along her body, relieved to feel her own skin. But then she panicked.

"Louis! Oh God, what happened to you?" She felt around in the dark but couldn't see him anywhere. "So much pain! How could you—"

The flick of his Zippo lighter caused her to spin around and see the halo from the flame illuminate his face, twisted in anger. "How could I what? Take drugs basically from a prostitute? Be so desperate? How could I what, Party Girl?"

"How could you live with so much pain? What happened to you? Why—"

"When your mum dies during your childhood and your father is a bloody alcoholic who likes to beat on you and throw you down the stairs, you become injured. You don't show anybody the pain, or else you get it worse the next time. And when you don't show anybody the pain, you don't receive medical care. Simple as that, Party Girl. I was a throwaway kid who scraped enough pennies together to run away to America with his band and reach for stardom, much like *your* Bones, however, no one helped us. We were totally on our own, making it. So forgive me if I'm having a hard time feeling sympathy for you or that pathetic lot you call friends. You probably never went without a day in your whole life."

Maggie's jaw hung open. The picture he so vividly painted of his life hurt worse, so much worse, than the feeling of crashing through the windshield of Thomas's car. She had seconds of pain. He'd had years.

"You did what you had to do, Louis. I don't blame you for any of it. No one could survive in that much pain without help. I'm just sorry your search for relief sealed your fate."

Louis had turned his back on Maggie during his tirade. He stood motionless. The light flared from his cigarette every so often so Maggie could still see where he was.

"Y-yes, well. Now you know and y-y-you won't need t-t-to ask me any m-m-more questions, will you? Come on then. I think we have one more stop to make before we come up with a game plan."

"A game plan? As in we actually get to do something? Finally!" She hurried to catch up with Louis. He didn't speak but she could feel his eyes on her as they trudged through gradually lightening darkness.

THE SMELL OF ENGINE OIL PERMEATED THE FOG UNTIL SHE FOUND HERSELF standing in front of Star's uncle's place in Houma. She recognized it from the times she'd gone out there with Devon and their daddy to work on Rose, Devon's classic Dodge Challenger. She heard loud sounds coming from the upstairs loft in the barn and headed that way. Louis caught her arm and turned her to face him.

"I just want to warn you," he said softly, then closed his mouth. He looked away as if to concentrate on putting his thoughts into the right words, but that wasn't necessary. Maggie already felt a sense of doom.

"Thanks, but I think I know."

He nodded slowly, his gray eyes so sad that she dreaded what awaited her at the top of the steps. The banging grew to a deafening volume as she climbed to the top of the ladder.

Before her, set in the center of the hayloft, was Star's original dilapidated drum set. Star was perched behind the kit, banging away.

His face was red from exertion and sweat covered his shirtless body. He paused in his drumming to hit play on a recorder he had set up next to him. The sounds of Devon's guitar filled the space as Star picked up the tempo. He pounded furiously on his skins, his face a mask of concentration.

Suddenly, he kicked his hi-hat over and screamed, "Fuck!" He jumped up off of his stool and kicked it backwards, then he grabbed his snare and threw it against the wall, breaking the plastic bits into tiny pieces.

Star sank to the floor, despondent. As Maggie approached, she saw piles and piles of beer bottles lying around the space and a sad excuse for a mattress with rumpled blankets and clothes all over. Star pulled at his hair, cursing to himself. He buried his face in his hands and let out the most gut-wrenching sob Maggie had ever heard.

Fuck the rules, Maggie thought to herself. She sat down on the floor next to Star and gathered him up in her arms. He clung to her as he cried his eyes out. Incomprehensible words spilled from his lips...names mostly. The names of his loved ones he had isolated himself from.

Maggie held on tight, willing as much of her essence as possible into this space she occupied so that he'd know he was not alone.

"I can't do this anymore," he cried against Maggie's shoulder. "Help me, please. I feel like I'm going to die, Maggie. Please."

Maggie stroked his shoulder and rocked him until he passed out in her arms. Louis appeared at her side and wordlessly helped her pick him up off of the floor and carried him over to his makeshift bed. She sat next to him on the awful mattress and stroked his hair, praying hard for him as he fell into a fitful sleep.

She heard the clink of glass and turned to see Louis cleaning up all of the beer bottles. Stunned, she watched him as he threw away every last one of them, including the full bottles in the half-empty case. He carried the garbage bags down the ladder carefully, making three trips. He righted the drum set, and then dug around in a pile of equipment until he found another snare and new heads for Star's remaining drums.

He changed every one of them and tuned the drums effortlessly. Maggie couldn't tear her eyes away from him. Once he finished the drums, he set the rest of the living space to rights. Finally he plopped down on Star's stool and looked around at the work he'd done. When his eyes met Maggie's, he frowned. "What?"

"You sure know your way around a drum set. Do you play and sing?"

Louis shrugged. "Some." He fingered the sticks Star had left in his holder. "Was that their music he was playing along to?" His tone was very quiet.

"Yeah, but I haven't heard that before. Perhaps it was something they came up with after...you know."

Louis nodded and leaned over to press play on the machine again. The sounds of her boys filled the room and her soul swooned at the amazing notes she heard. Whatever this was, it was incredibly powerful. It sounded like them, but different. More grown up.

She and Louis sat there and listened to the entire tape. When it stopped, Louis nodded. He poked around a bit, seemingly not quite sure how to work the machine, before the lid popped up and he could pull out the cassette.

"Its got writing on it. It says 'Haunted Demos'. Does that make any sense to you?"

Maggie shrugged. "I'm not sure. They must have done another album after I was gone."

A cell phone rang from under the pile of clothes on the bed. Maggie looked to Louis, who gestured for her to join him in a dark corner of the loft. Star sat up slowly, rubbing his eyes as he reached for the phone.

"Bro, you alright? Ain't heard a word in some time."

It was good to hear Jade's voice. Star felt as if he'd been hit over the head with something, kinda like when Mackenzie let her mallet slip while tenderizing a steak and it hit him upside the face. God, Mackenzie...

"How's my favorite college boy?" Star asked, trying not to sound as despondent as he felt. He looked around at his bed, wondering how he'd gotten there. He'd been drinking so much lately, there were gaps in his memory. Just like before.

"Star?"

"Yeah, sorry. I just… I'm having a weird night."

Jade was quiet for a moment on the other end of the phone. "There's been a lot of that shit going on lately. Have you talked to the other guys?"

Star could barely focus on the voice. His vision was clearing enough that he could see someone had been there. His shit was all cleaned up.

Then he remembered.

"Dude! I'm coming out there. You don't sound right."

Star shook himself. This was his chance. If he didn't reach out for help now…

"I'm not doing so good, my friend."

"Hang tight. I'm on my way."

"WHAT THE FUCK IS YOUR PROBLEM?!" MACKENZIE SCREAMED AS SHE yanked her door open. "Oh. Oops. Sorry, Jade. I've been trying to do the books for the shop for the last hour and I've gotten like eight calls, a zillion texts, and the shit they're playing across the street has me wanting to throw dead cats at them. Come on in!"

Jade chuckled as he passed Mackenzie to enter her apartment. "I totally agree about the music. Lately they've had some of the strangest bands play. I don't even know what you'd call some of it. I was trying to study for my finals the other night and it was so loud… Anyway. I'm sorry to bother you, but I need you to come with me."

Mackenzie raised an eyebrow at him and crossed her arms over her chest. Jade knew he was about to get a ration of shit from his hotheaded neighbor, but he also knew if anyone could reach Star, it was her.

The day the band had come to meet the "tattoo girl" in the shop below, Star had instead made a beeline for Mackenzie. He'd instantly hit it off with the flamboyant woman and easily fell into a comfortable, if a bit tumultuous, relationship.

The truth was, she scared Jade a little, but Star was completely enamored with her. Things were great between them, even when they had to be apart, until the band split. She'd tried to be there for him, but she had her own issues and lost patience with him when he fell off the wagon. His depression was dragging them both down, so he started staying away more frequently. They never actually broke up, at least not that Jade knew of, but something was broken between them.

"If it's about Star, then you're wasting your time. He doesn't want to see me. He made that perfectly clear when he decided to ignore my calls. Whatever. I can't help someone who doesn't want to be helped. I got enough shit to deal with on my own." Her words were harsh, but Jade noticed the tears brimming in her big blue eyes.

"He asked, chère. Please?"

She blinked hard and looked away for a minute.

"Fine. Give me five minutes. We're taking my truck, though. I'm not riding that death trap you call transportation in this freezing-ass cold!" She stomped off to her room while Jade fought a snicker. He took the time to call Mage and Devon and tell them what was going on. They agreed to meet at Devon's house in Houma. They were supposed to be there for Christmas Eve the day after tomorrow anyway. The party was just going to start early, it seemed.

MAGGIE STIRRED NEXT TO LOUIS. HE'D TUCKED THE TWO OF THEM INTO A corner and used a little of his talents to make her fall asleep, or at least fall into a relaxed state. He did it as much for himself as for her. He needed time to process what had just happened.

Star was so much like him. He recognized the scenario as if it had come from one of his own nightmares. Alone in a hovel, feeling so disconnected you can't even pick up a phone and call someone. He knew their timing was crucial. Star didn't have much time. Watching him pace around the loft, pulling at his hair, Louis recognized the signs. If his friends didn't get here soon, he'd wake Maggie and they'd keep him here. This bloke was so close to punching his ticket.

Louis looked down at Maggie's relaxed face and couldn't help himself. He brushed his fingers down her cheek, something he'd been telling himself not to do the more time they spent together. He took one of her bouncy curls between his fingers and shuddered at the silky feel.

In rest, she was still radiant. She was all of the goodness Louis had never seen in his own screwed up existence rolled up into one beautiful woman, one he was fighting an attraction to that went beyond her pretty face. She was so good to everyone. Even him, bastard that he was. That kind of goodness drew people in, was drawing *him* in, and he didn't have the energy to resist any longer.

Without regard for his sanity or his fate, he leaned closer, inhaling her lingering scent. She'd broken through his defenses completely with her performance with Star. *Why couldn't I have had someone to hold me as she held this man, her friend? Why discover her now when time is all but up for me?*

"Louis," Maggie moaned softly. She shifted, pressing herself closer to him. They were practically in a lover's embrace and Louis panicked. He couldn't fight the urge to kiss her for much longer. He was not that strong. Her eyes slowly opened and quickly went wide with surprise— then narrowed dangerously, as if she was ready to pounce.

A woman's voice called from below. "Star? Baby? Are you up there?"

Star broke out in a cold sweat at the sound of Mackenzie's voice. She was going to be so pissed when she saw him. He knew he was a mess. He looked around, ready to hide his disaster zone, and then remembered it was clean. Who cleaned up his shit?

"Jade, if you keep looking up my skirt, you're going to get this boot heel in the middle of that pretty forehead of yours!"

"I'm sorry! I'm not trying, chère! It's just—"

"Can it, schoolboy. STAR!" She made it up to the top of the ladder and attempted to step gracefully onto the platform. Words left Star completely at the sight of his beloved. She ran to him and threw her arms around his neck, pulling him tightly against her.

"Oh, dammit. Baby! You're so thin! Star—" He tried to pull back from her but she held on. "No fucking way. Uh-uh. You listen to me, Stanley Stevenson! Enough is enough!"

"Kenz," Jade warned. "Hey, brother." He stepped over and looked to Mackenzie to give them a moment. The two men hugged and Jade winced when he felt his friend's emaciated frame against him.

"I was playing tonight, you know? I was trying to play the stuff we did on the last album, just to keep it fresh in case...well... And I can't do it. I can't feel it anymore. The music, Jade." He pulled away from Jade and started pacing again.

"I can't do this anymore," he whispered before sinking down to the floor. "For a minute tonight I felt like Maggie was here. I'm totally losing my shit, dude. I need to go away. If I don't go away, I'm..."

MAGGIE STIRRED NEXT TO HIM AT THE SOUND OF THEIR VOICES.

"Okay, Louis. This is bullshit. I can't stand this. They can't lose Star. He can't..."

She slumped against Louis once more. He knew she'd seen enough. It was time for action, and for the first time, Louis felt compelled to be a part of the solution.

SIX

"I THINK THIS IS A BAD IDEA," MARCUS SAID FOR THE FIFTIETH TIME.

Sherry rolled her eyes as she turned the rental car down the street her GPS said led to Devon's house in Houma.

"You need to think positive," she said, feeling a little unsure herself. Jaylene and Sammara had called her yesterday and insisted the two of them come out to Louisiana.

"Sherry, if we don't do something now, this is it. It'll be over for good." Sammara had told her she'd seen that something terrible was going to happen, and when she told Mage, he freaked out.

The guys were all falling apart. It was up to their women to put them back together. It would take the four of them to try to exert even one iota of the influence Maggie had had on them.

"They aren't going to want to see me," Marcus muttered. He'd been really restless as the second anniversary of Maggie's death had passed without any sort of olive branch from his brothers. He said it was time to completely move on, but Sherry wouldn't let him, not without a fight.

"So what? If one of them was in need, you'd be there in a heartbeat. That's what we're doing here. One of your brothers needs you, so we came. Simple as that. At least talk to them. If you guys can't work the business out, then so be it. You've got your solo album coming together and we'll be fine. But they're your family, your history. Let's give it one more try, okay? Mr. Lambert?"

She hoped a little teasing would loosen him up. She saw him smirk out of the corner of her eye.

"If you say so, Mrs. Lambert. Anything for you, my beautiful wife. By the way, they're probably going to shit when they find out we got married. Well, maybe. They may not even give a shit—"

"Marcus, honey. Don't think like that." She really hoped she could trust her girlfriends that she wasn't leading him into a disaster. He'd never healed from their breakup, and if this went badly, he likely never would.

She pulled in the driveway and recognized Mackenzie's truck, Sammara's Ford Escape, and Devon's Challenger parked alongside the house. The sky was gray and was threatening to storm. From what she'd heard, that tended to happen when they were under this roof together. She shivered as they approached the walk and said a silent prayer that this reunion be a positive one.

Marie Doucette Boudreaux opened the front door, leaning on her cane, and simply beamed at the sight of her estranged nephew. She held out her other hand and said, "Come here, my boy. Let me hug on you."

Marcus bent down and kissed his aunt's frail cheek. He mentally kicked himself that he hadn't been to see her throughout her treatment. He'd sent flowers monthly and had called her a couple of times, but those were pathetic gestures compared to all the times she'd been there for him.

"I've missed you, Aunt Marie," he said quietly in her ear. He choked back a sob, trying to keep it together. He couldn't lose it now, not when he had to be strong enough to take whatever his brothers were going to give him.

"And I you," Marie replied. She smiled warmly at Sherry and took her hand. "So good of you to bring him here, my dear."

Sherry kissed her cheek and looked to Marcus. "It's about time, am I right?" She raised an eyebrow and gave an "mmm hmmm" to Marcus before walking past him to enter the house.

He shook his head at her attitude, but it comforted him. He knew she'd be in his corner no matter what went down tonight.

They entered the living room to find Jade and Mage decorating a gigantic Christmas tree. Mage was on his tiptoes, trying to place a star on a high branch.

"D, you should be doing this part. You're taller than this fucker. I can't reach that high."

"Ha! See? I'm not the only one who thinks you're as tall as a tree," Jaylene said. "Thank goodness. I never have to climb up on the counters to get to my top cabinets anymore," she teased. He smacked her on the butt and she jumped out of reach for a second swat. She carried some more ornaments over to Mage, who took them with a smile.

Star and Mackenzie were sitting together quietly on the loveseat, barely touching or looking at each other. He looked like absolute shit. Marcus knew the feeling. He'd been there himself. He squeezed Sherry's hand for support as Marie announced their arrival.

"Boys and girls. Marcus and Sherry are here."

Seven pairs of eyes turned and focused on the couple in the doorway.

Everyone went quiet. No one moved. Not until Devon stood and approached them. He glanced at Marcus, then took Sherry's hand, bending to kiss her on the cheek.

"Thank you both for coming," he said. He stood before Marcus and offered him his hand. Marcus swallowed hard and placed his hand in Devon's, surprised at the grip. He stumbled as Devon pulled him in for a bro hug and pounded on his back.

He blinked to clear his eyes from tears in time to see Mage step up behind Devon. He greeted Sherry with a smile and a kiss on the cheek, then stood before Marcus with an intense look on his face.

"I see you, bro."

Marcus nodded as he shook hands with Mage. Star waved from where he was sitting, but made no move to greet him. Fair enough.

"Hi, Marcus," Jade said with emotion.

Marcus nearly cracked at the sight of his little brother. He'd completely changed his look. Marcus couldn't tell if he was still angry with him. Jade's mistrust hurt most of all. Not that he'd ever given Jade a reason to trust him. It was just something he'd always counted on.

"Little brother. How's college?" Marcus had never been this nervous or uncomfortable in his life. Sherry nudged him to get him to move farther into the room.

"Can I take your coats, kids?"

"I got it, Mama," Devon said. He took Sherry's coat and then Marcus's, giving him a nod as he made his way toward the back of the house.

Sherry led the stiff-as-a-board Marcus over to the sofa. She had to push him to sit down, as if he didn't have control over his rigid limbs. Marcus then watched as Sherry hugged Sammara and Jaylene, then made her way over to Mackenzie, who stood and hugged her for a long time.

"Star? I hope you're okay with us being here," Sherry said quietly, taking his hand. He shook it limply.

Star chewed on a fingernail and rubbed at his hair. "I'm cool." He so was not okay. Mackenzie had told Sherry he hadn't even wanted to come tonight, but Mackenzie insisted. Things were really tense between them. He was afraid and needed support. Mackenzie had said she was afraid she couldn't handle the kind of support he needed.

"College is great," Jade said, drawing Marcus' attention away from the sorrowful scene. "I took my finals last week and got A's in all of my courses." Everyone congratulated him and he beamed proudly. He answered everyone's questions, which filled up the tense silence until dinner was ready.

Everyone moved to the table and took their seats, with Devon at one end and Marie at the other. Jaylene and Sammara brought out all of the food dishes and serving utensils.

"You guys mind if I say a blessing?" Mage asked the group. They all nervously held hands. They closed their eyes and listened quietly as Mage said a prayer combining their Catholic background, Sammara's Wiccan beliefs, and the Voodoo he'd learned from Gran. When it was finished, they all began serving themselves.

Talk during dinner covered the safe topics: How renovations of the St. Germaine were going, how Sammara was enjoying living in New Orleans, how things were going at the shop for Jaylene and Sammara. No one discussed the elephant in the room. Marcus waited anxiously for a bomb to go off.

MAGGIE AWOKE FROM SOME SORT OF SLUMBER TO FIND HERSELF SNUGGLED up to Louis's shoulder. Surprised that he would allow her to get so close, she didn't make a move. She merely stared up into his handsome, yet vulnerable face. She was fascinated by his throat, how the Adam's apple stood out so prominently. His jawline was arrogant and the crease in his chin, what her mama always called God's thumbprint, was dramatic. His lips were so full and pink they gave him a constant pouty look. A nose long and straight was covered with a light sprinkling of freckles. Eyebrows jutted out dramatically, giving an air of contempt. Maggie imagined that a full smile from him would destroy her.

She couldn't help the attraction she felt to him, although she questioned whether it was because she was curious about him and determined to win him over, or just because he was a warm body in a cold, cold place.

Louis swallowed. "I believe you're playing possum, Party Girl."

Maggie giggled at his phrase. "Maybe. Or maybe I'm just dreaming."

His lips quirked up into a smirk. "Either way, I do believe I've come up with a plan. Your kin have gathered at someone named Marie's home and are having Christmas Eve dinner. I let you rest while I analyzed our options."

He paused in his speech, likely waiting for Maggie to respond, but she had been too busy listening to his voice rumble through his chest. She was enthralled watching his lips move.

"EARTH TO MAGGIE? ARE YOU WITH ME?" LOUIS WAS GROWING increasingly uncomfortable. He realized moments before that he'd been stroking her hip absently with the hand attached to the arm he had around her. He couldn't exactly yank his arm away or she'd know he'd let his guard down. But then he glanced down into her clear blue eyes and got a little lost. She was way too close. She shouldn't be looking at him like that, as though she wanted him to kiss her.

"What happens when we finish whatever it is that we have to do? What's going to happen to us?" She blinked her beautiful eyes and suddenly Louis wanted to take her fears away. He didn't know why, but it became apparent that he wasn't willing to give her up. Not yet. Not that she was his in the first place. She was his charge, but not *his*. He'd lost hope he would ever have anything that was his.

"It's different for everybody. Didn't the old woman explain that to you?"

Maggie frowned and fidgeted, which caused her body to brush even more against Louis's hypersensitive one.

"She said I'd have to make a choice. Something about destiny. I don't know what that means, and I hate that. I fully understand that I can't go back to the way things were. My life is over. But I'm not done living. Do you know what I mean?"

He was doing it again! His thumb traced over where he should have felt the side elastic of her knickers. There was nothing. He remembered her earlier confession. *Bloody hell.*

"All I can tell you is that remaining in Purgatory is a special sort of torture. Listening to all of those newly dead, blah blah blah. It's pathetic."

"Then why were you still there? Why haven't you moved on?"

Louis thought about that long and hard. Then he laughed, surprising Maggie.

"I haven't a clue! It seemed like the cheeky thing to do in the beginning, refusing to go along with the program. That's what I do, what I've always done. Fat lot of good it's done me. I think I kind of like giving the finger to the Old Chap upstairs. It's the only bit of fun I've got left."

MAGGIE CHUCKLED AND SNUGGLED CLOSER TO HIM, NOT READY TO GIVE UP this feeling. Intimacy. His laughter had been music to her ears. She felt as thought she were finally getting through to him.

"You sound like me. I was frequently known to do things just to spite the man. It's a good thing I'm smart or I would have lost my career before it even started. You have to be quick on your feet in my business, or they run all over you."

"You mean you *had* to be quick. Maggie, do you really understand that it's over? I don't want this for you, this eternal nothingness." His other hand came up to cup her jaw. "You deserve a much better afterlife."

Touched by his concern, Maggie covered his hand with hers. "And what about you? You can't go on pissing off the dude in charge just for shits and giggles! Don't you want to find some peace?"

Louis leaned back and closed his eyes. "I'm just so tired. I wouldn't know what peace was if it came right up and shook me hand. I can't even imagine it."

Maggie placed her hand on his chest, over his still heart. "What brought you happiness when you were alive?"

Louis exhaled long and hard. "Music. That's all I ever had. It might have been rubbish, but it was mine. I had plans, you know. Punk gave me my break, but there was so much more. I went out to the desert to record with my band and I was exposed to so much more than punk. I had all of these new songs running around in my head. But I couldn't... The pain was so much. I just gave up." He closed his eyes and his eyebrows pulled together in a grimace. "I just wanted it to stop. Just for a little while," he whispered.

"If you could have any afterlife you wanted, what would you choose for yourself?" Maggie asked.

"A life of curing stupidity."

Maggie barked out a laugh at his words.

"I'm being serious," he said, his lip quirking, betraying his amusement. "If I could go around and give a little metaphysical smack upside the head to all of the idiots in the world, maybe I'd get a bit of fun out of it."

"Okay, that's one option," Maggie agreed. "But what do you want for *you*? What would make you feel whole?"

Louis' hand was now stroking Maggie's that sat upon his chest. If he thought about it, he'd freak out and throw her off of him, but he couldn't help himself. It was as though Maggie was the sun breaking through the clouds after a rainstorm. The rays of light touched him inside and he knew if he just waited, just a bit more, he'd feel warm for once in his miserable life. Or undeath. Whatever this was. God, why did she have to smell so alluring? And her curves under his hands were so tempting. And her husky voice, as though she'd been singing the blues all night long in some dive bar full of cigarette smoke and sorrow.

"Music. And someone to share it with." He'd never admitted his loneliness to anyone before. Why now? Why, when he knew he couldn't have her…

SEVEN

Maggie and Louis resurfaced suddenly in a very familiar dining room. Maggie covered her mouth with both hands and fought back the urge to cry out.

"Let's not let them know we're here yet, love. This is a critical event. We're about to see what needs to be seen."

Maggie frowned up at Louis. "Are you shitting me? You're going to talk like Grandma now?" She cursed to herself, trying not to alert Mage or his lady friend to her presence. She turned her attention to the table.

"I'd like to make a toast," Marie announced to the group. "It's been too long since I've had all my boys, and their lovely ladies of course, under this roof. I know it's been a rough year, but we're here, and I..." She trailed off, her eyes brimming with tears.

Jade clinked glasses loudly with Mage, startling them all. That led to an awkward moment during which they all clinked glasses together and hushed "cheers" were spoken. Couples looked at each other. Marcus tried not to make eye contact with anyone but Sherry, his eyes full of emotion.

"I think..." Jaylene said, interrupting the murmurs. She stood at her seat next to Devon, who was at one end of the table frowning. "I think what needs to be said is that there is a lot of tension here. I'm going to put it out there that I'd really like to see you guys talk to each other."

Maggie was pleased to see Jaylene take the reins here. She just hoped it was enough to get these knuckleheads talking.

"I know it's not easy," Jaylene continued, "but you've come back from worse, and I can't just shoot paintballs at you this time," she said with a nervous laugh. "I just can't stand to see you all in pain when we could all be supporting each other through—"

"Jaylene, I appreciate what you are trying to do," Jade said with a sad smile. "The problem is that trust has been broken and I'm just not sure how to fix it. We've been through a lot, and some people—"

"Some people?" Marcus barked out a laugh. "Let's just tell it like it is, little bro. I'm the problem. End of story. Aunt Marie," he said, standing from the table. "I'm sorry my being here has caused problems for your meal. We'll go. Merry Christmas everyone." He reached for Sherry's hand, but she remained sitting. He looked at her questioningly. "Babe?"

"No." She stood calmly from her chair and put her hands on his shoulders. "I think it's time, you know, for you guys to—"

"Sherry? Please. Both of you sit down," Devon said, his voice firm. Maggie was pleased to see him take charge from the place their daddy once sat.

"Jaylene and Sherry are right," he continued. "This has gone on too long. Maggie would want us to mend fences. At the very least, we should be able to sit around a fucking table without giving each other the stink-eye."

Oh enough of this, Maggie thought to herself. She looked at Louis and he nodded. It was time.

Sammara giggled and then covered her mouth. "I'm sorry. Terribly inappropriate." Mage turned to look at her in surprise.

At that moment, Sammara gasped and her head dropped back.

"Chère! What—"

Maggie gasped for air and slowly raised her head to look at the others. She felt just like when she'd been in Louis's memory, but this was happening for real. She was in Sammara's body.

"Fuck!" Jade shouted. "Mage! What the fuck—"

"Really, Jade?" Maggie asked with a laugh. "That's all you got to say? Come on, boys and girls. Let's all sit down like grown-ups and work this out. I've had about enough of this nonsense." Maggie's words coming out of Sammara sounded strange to her ears. It was eerie…not quite hers.

"Sammara, honey, are you feeling okay?" Mackenzie asked, her blue eyes wide. Star cleared his throat and brought shaky hands to the table.

Maggie turned her head to look at Mackenzie and the group gasped.

"Your eyes," Jaylene murmured in awe. Maggie looked in the mirror on the wall to her left and raised an eyebrow.

All of the white was gone. Her eyes, well, Sammara's eyes, were completely black. *Huh.*

Maggie stood from the table carefully, getting used to the way this body worked. She tossed her hair back, and walked with a bounce over to Jade. She squeezed his shoulder. She turned and smiled at Mackenzie.

"I got this," she then said with a wink. She looked to Star and said, "Don't I always got this?"

"Holy shit," Jade breathed. "Maggie. It *is* you."

"Stop fucking around," Devon said, rising slowly from his chair to his full height. "Sammara, if you're fucking around, I swear to God…"

Mage stood and approached Maggie cautiously. "Chère, where did we go for Samhain that year you—"

Maggie turned on Mage with a wicked smile, cutting him off.

"Congo Square! Duh!" She rolled her eyes and walked over to Marie. She took her mother's hands in hers and bit her lip.

"Mama, I'm sorry to do this, but I gotta have my boys together. This just ain't gonna work for me."

Marie's blue eyes watered and she reached up to touch Sammara's face. "Maggie," she whispered.

Maggie nodded.

Marcus approached them just in time to catch a fainting Marie. He carefully laid Marie on the floor as Jaylene hurried to her side. She took her pulse.

"She's okay," she whispered, looking around with wide eyes.

Devon stomped over to the other end of the table. "I've had just about enough—"

"All of you sit down," Maggie spoke with authority, her voice deepening into a husky tone more like her own than Sammara's. "I don't have much time," she said. "I can't believe you let almost a year go by with all of you such a mess. Jaylene, Sherry...I'm grateful for all you've done to keep my boys together, but this bullshit right here? Enough. Star?"

Star wrapped his arms around himself and started rocking in the chair. "This isn't happening. I've totally lost it. Oh God." His face went white and he started chewing on a nail.

"Hey," Mackenzie said to him, touching his hand. "This shit is real. I don't know what the fuck is going on, but I'm starting to feel like we're in some fucked-up Charles Dickens play. Mage? Your girl over there—"

"Sammara ain't here right now, Kenz," Mage said, standing motionless. "It don't smell like her. It don't sound like her. It sounds like—"

"Can we move on, please?" Maggie said impatiently. "Look. Marcus is a disrespectful buttmunch, but you've all fucked up at one point or another. I *know* you all know that. Do we need to mention the release party?" The guilty faces around her let her know she had their attention.

"It's time you put your egos aside and remember that you have built something together because you all fucking love each other. Enough's enough. All of you feel like something's missing because the Bones are defunct. What the hell is it going to take for you jackasses to accept things as they are? I'm not coming back. Sherry was doing a helluva job managing you. You all have more music to make together. If you need time off, by all means. Do what you gotta do. But none of you are leaving this house until you've all mended fences. It's my job to mind you. It always has been. I can't take your pain one more minute or I'm going to start knocking skulls together, you hear me?"

Jade reached up to rub his shoulder. "It was you in my class. You wrote in my book."

Maggie smiled at him and pointed. "At least this guy's paying attention."

Mage frowned. "I know you were in the cemetery on All Saints'. But why?"

LOUIS STEPPED FORWARD OUT OF THE SHADOWS AND THE ENTIRE ROOM gasped.

"Sorry to interrupt this little love-in, but you all need to listen to Maggie and listen good. One of you in this room will not live past the week if you don't sort yourselves out tonight. Grow some fucking bollocks, say what you need to say, and get on with it. I have to take her back soon."

Maggie felt a hand on the shoulder of her borrowed body. She turned to find her beloved brother standing before her. She looked up into his eyes and wanted to cry, but she had to be strong. She had their attention. She put a hand up to his cheek.

"You always were so damn tall." His face screwed up like he was trying to fight back the tears. Maggie couldn't fall apart now.

"Maggie...I'm so sorry..."

Devon stood there looking just as he had the day they'd buried their father.

"You have nothing to apologize for. We all made bad decisions. Sadly, mine hurt you all more than I could know. It's over now. You all have to move on without me. Nothing I can do about that. But if you don't take care of each other, everything you've built together, everything *we* built, will vanish. I love you all too much to see that happen."

Maggie felt a pull and she panicked. She grabbed for Devon, but her hands wouldn't grasp...

"PARTY GIRL," LOUIS SAID CLOSE TO HER EAR. "OUR TIME IS UP."

He saw her fear in her eyes before she grabbed her brother using Sammara's body. Devon caught her weight as Sammara fell against him— and Maggie ended up limp in Louis's arms.

He turned to look at the others, who were still staring at him cradling her to his chest. Devon stepped forward, but Louis shook his head.

"Right. It's time for Maggie to move on, otherwise she'll be stuck in Purgatory for good. Promise her now you will do as she asks and mend yourselves. Let her hear you before we go."

"Tell them to take care of Star," Maggie mumbled. "If they lose him..."

Louis looked around and caught Mage's eye.

"I heard. I see you, Maggie," he said in a broken voice. All eyes fell on Star, who was still rocking back and forth, crying softly in his chair.

Maggie made eye contact with Jaylene. Before she vanished, she whispered, "Take care of them. You got this."

Jaylene, still kneeling next to Marie, nodded slightly.

Maggie looked up into the only thing she had to hold on to. A pair of gray eyes full of...

"Well, that was unexpected," Marcus said, surveying the damage.

Marie was starting to come around. Devon passed an unconscious Sammara into Mage's arms so he could carry her over to the couch near the Christmas tree.

Sherry stood by Marcus, squeezing his hand for support. "I don't even know what to say," she said, feeling as though her entire foundation had been shaken.

Marcus put his arm around her and smiled sadly. "I think it's time for—"

"Us to apologize. Brother," Jade said, approaching his older brother slowly. "We have things to discuss. All of us. Like," he said, gesturing to their hands together and their matching wedding bands. "Were you going to tell us that you two got married?"

All eyes landed on the couple, who moved closer together as if they wished they would be swallowed up.

"Yeah, well, I can explain..."

"It sounds like we all have some 'splainin' to do," Mackenzie muttered.

EIGHT

MAGGIE SAT UPRIGHT AND FOUND HERSELF BACK IN THE DINGY GYMNASIUM. The circle of chairs was empty except for her and Grandma.

"Louis! Where's—"

"The time has come for you to—"

"Wait! You can't...I just need to speak to Louis. Please. Can I have five minutes? Please?"

Grandma smiled knowingly and looked toward the double doors, now illuminated. They flew open with a loud clang that echoed through the room. Maggie's undead heart fluttered in her chest. He walked towards her smoking a cigarette. He took a seat two chairs over from her in the circle and looked to Grandma.

Grandma looked between the two of them and then spoke to Maggie. "You have five minutes." She stood and walked into the blackness.

Maggie turned on her chair. Louis glanced down, suddenly very interested in his fingernails.

"So what happened? What—"

"We did what we needed to do. Case closed." He refused to make eye contact with her. His hair fell forward, but she could still see his mouth as he spoke. His lip trembled.

"Louis? Is this what you do? Just go around and help people like me?"

He shrugged his wide shoulders. "I suppose. Although this was quite an adventure, wasn't it?" A small smile touched his lips for the briefest moment and then was gone.

Maggie wasn't ready to move on. Plain and simple. There was still too much unspoken between them. If that meant she had to handcuff herself to this man, so be it.

"So how does one get a gig like yours? Hmmm? I think helping people on their way, helping people who need minding, helping the living deal with their grief… It's kind of a nice racket, don't you think?"

Louis slowly turned his head to look at Maggie as though she'd gone completely mental. "What in hell are you saying? You want to stay like this? Forever? You'd give up an existence free from worry and fear for your loved ones? To continue—"

"I thought we made a pretty good team," Maggie said, crossing her legs and looking down at her own nails. She glanced up to see Louis staring longingly at her legs. Maggie had never been hesitant about using whatever tools she had, within reason, to get what she wanted.

Louis turned towards her and leaned his arm over the back of his chair. "What makes you think I'd want to be stuck with you, Party Girl?" His words didn't sting near enough and the faint smile and flicker of excitement in his eyes told her she was about to seal the deal.

"Because," she said sliding over onto the chair next to him. He couldn't hide the smile creeping onto his face. "You need someone to keep you entertained, someone to mind *you*. Someone with…I don't know…" Maggie leaned towards Louis and reached out a finger. "A woman's touch?"

NINE

LOUIS HELD HIS UN-BREATH. COULD SHE POSSIBLY MEAN IT?

"You must be a g-glutton f-f-for punishment," Louis stammered, kicking himself at the return of his damn stutter. His every attempt to control her had failed, all because of his stutter.

"Maybe," she said, blowing her hair up out of her eyes. "But then again, I think this could be fun! You said you wanted to cure stupidity! Maybe we can! Ooo and maybe we can make people fall in looooove."

Louis shook his head. Hopeless. She was hopeless. *He* was hopeless over her. She'd grown on him and, sick as it sounded, he didn't want her to move on. How selfish! How could he wish this existence on her?

But really, it wasn't that bad now, was it? Especially not with the way she smiled up at him, the way she let her shoe hang from her toes, accentuating the curve of her instep... She was intoxicating to be around. And infuriating.

"What makes you think we have any say in what we do?"

"Because! Look at we just did! Those boys are so pigheaded, and we got them to talk to each other! If we can work that magic, just think of what we could do if we put our heads together!"

Or parts farther south, Louis thought to himself. Sick bastard that he was, he couldn't help himself. He wanted her desperately. He didn't even know if that sort of thing worked anymore. Could dead people actually have sex? He'd seen some crazy things in the places he'd been, and he knew that they were basically tangible beings who existed on another plane. The physics were kind of inexplicable, so he didn't spend much time wondering about it. All he cared about was that the physical pain he'd felt most of his life was non-existent. It was the cold that permeated everything that bothered him from time-to-time, reminding him of his childhood in England.

Maggie chased that cold away. Being with her made him feel more alive than he'd ever felt. She could easily become his new drug if he wasn't careful.

"So where do we go first?" she asked, as if it were a done deal. He chuckled to himself. She just decided and that's that?

Grandma re-entered the gymnasium and shuffled toward them, smiling broadly.

"Margaret, dear. It's time for you to make your choice."

"Great. I'm staying with Louis."

Grandma raised her eyebrows. "That's not—"

"Oh come on, Grandma. You know it's a great idea! Louis is a little rough around the edges, don't you think? A woman's touch would just add that certain…"

Grandma shifted her surprised gaze to Louis. He held up his hands.

"Don't look at me. I didn't create this monster."

Grandma looked between them and then closed her eyes for a moment. Louis waited with bated breath for her response. Before he knew what he was doing, he found himself sending up a little prayer to the Old Chap.

Just let me have a little more time with her. I know she's too good for me, but she makes it all better. If I could just spend… Just a few more tasks and then she can move on to her afterlife where she'll be free. I just want her to be happy. Please—

"Very well then. You have permission to work together until such a time as—"

"Thank you, Grandma," Maggie said as she launched herself at the old woman and gave her an enthusiastic hug. Grandma chuckled and patted her on the back.

"Louis will remain our contact and will be given instructions. Margaret, you must listen to—"

"Yeah, I got it," Maggie said as she tugged Louis up to his feet. He was shocked at her behavior. No one talked to Grandma like that. Grandma seemed a little taken aback as well.

"She's your responsibility," Grandma said gravely to him. Louis swallowed hard. He hoped he wouldn't fail.

"I understand," he said quietly. Maggie was bouncing on her toes with excitement as she clutched his arm tightly.

"Well, Party Girl, it appears you get your wish. Come on, then," he said as they walked away from the circle and into the darkness. He pulled out a cigarette and lit it with shaky hands, wondering just what the hell he'd gotten himself into.

"So where do we go first?" She slid her hand down his arm and linked fingers with him. Her hand felt so nice. He was grateful he didn't perspire any longer or his palms would have been drenched right now.

"We walk until we end up where we are meant to be. I hope those shoes aren't uncomfortable. We could be walking for some time."

"What do we do in between tasks? What do you usually do?"

Louis shrugged. "Dunno. Find a quiet place to sit near the water. Go and listen to some live music somewhere. But usually wherever I end up, there's a task to be completed. It just sort of happens."

Maggie kept quiet for a time and Louis enjoyed listening to her heels clack along and feeling her presence next to him. Thoughts and wonderings about her occupied his mind. He hoped she wouldn't be sorry she accompanied him and get—

"Wow, this is kind of boring," she said with a laugh, dashing Louis' hopes. What if she couldn't handle it? What if she—

"We should tell stories or Oooo! You should sing to me! I want to hear you sing, Louis. Sing me a song."

He stopped walking and dropped her hand. His first instinct was to cop an attitude and insult her. But then he found himself singing to her the first song that came to mind. "Ever Fallen In Love" never sounded so true! He didn't even move away when she linked her arm with his and snuggled close.

"The Buzzcocks! I love that song," Maggie said. "You have a fantastic voice! Oh my God, Louis. That's like some serious panty-melting stuff right there!"

Louis groaned inwardly. He tried to play off how much she affected him. "You don't wear panties, isn't that right?"

She looked up at him with a smirk. "You remembered. Are you still thinking about my panties, Louis?"

He shrugged. "Not really," he lied, refusing to make eye contact. "I often find undergarments to be too constricting myself." *Like now.* He was going to have the worst case of blue balls in history for the rest of eternity if she kept toying with him. "Although, if I were wearing a dress, I'd be concerned about catching a draft."

Idiot. He just confessed his perverted thoughts. She was going to know exactly what he was thinking about.

Maggie pulled him to a stop and turned him to face her. "If you want to know about my panties, you'll just have to find out for yourself." And then the damned woman kissed him.

Surprised, he stumbled back. What was she thinking? What was *he* thinking? He didn't dare turn down her invitation. Here was his opportunity to find out just how much a dead person could actually feel.

Maggie started to apologize, but he cut her off with his lips. Her slight body fit perfectly in his arms. Her thick hair provided a perfect grip. He pulled her so tightly to him, her ample breasts flattened against his chest. She moaned softly as he deepened the kiss, sliding a hand down to cup her ass and bring her bottom half just as close. *God* she felt good. The curve of her bottom filled his large hand perfectly. He wanted more. He hiked her leg up his side and was ready to support all of her weight and find a wall somewhere when he realized they were standing next to a park bench near the water and a very large dog was growling softly.

MAGGIE BROKE AWAY FIRST. "OOPS. UH, LOUIS? I THINK THAT DOG KNOWS we're here." She stumbled out of his hold and smoothed her dress down.

Lord, could this man kiss! Or ghost. Whatever. She wanted to scream! Talk about kissus-interruptus! She had a major lady boner for this man and was ready to hike up her dress and see if ghosts could really get down. Oh, and his hands! He really knew how to hold a woman, possess her...

"Nice doggie," Louis said, backing away slowly. The man on the bench called to his dog and it moved closer to him, still watching them out of the corner of its eye.

"Don't make any quick moves," Louis said as he wrapped an arm around her waist and pulled her backwards with him. Maggie frowned. He wasn't really afraid of this dog, was he?

"Louis," she whispered. "Why are you freaking out over this dog? Dead, remember? It's not like it could bite us." She fought a case of the giggles when she saw how afraid he looked.

"Of course I know that. I'm not stupid. I j-j-ju-just..."

Maggie knew not to push it. They'd put quite a bit of distance between them and the man and his dog. Louis was just starting to breathe normal.

"That was close. He's our next charge," he said. Maggie wondered how he knew and was about to ask when the man began to sing in a beautiful, heartwrenchingly soulful voice. It brought tears to her eyes and a hollow feeling to her chest just listening to him.

"That's amazing," she breathed.

Louis stiffened next to her. "He's had a terrible accident. We are to connect him with a woman..."

Maggie waited for him to continue, but his eyes were trained on some spot out in the middle of the water. She wasn't sure where they were, but it was some sort of bay.

"A woman? But where?"

Louis smirked in that way that made Maggie's toes curl. She was still waiting for his full smile, but that smirk certainly kept her intrigued.

He raised a finger and pointed out towards the middle of the water. "She's out there."

WANT TO READ MORE? EXCERPTS FOR RELATED STORIES FOLLOW THIS LETTER...

DEAR READERS

Thank you for continuing on this journey with me! After writing Haunted, I spent a lot of time thinking about Maggie and what happened to her. I wrote Fated next and really started to explore the idea of the connections between the living and deceased through writing Sammara's character. I was asked to be a part of a Paranormal Bad Boys anthology last fall, and since I hadn't really written much paranormal, I jumped at the opportunity to try something new. The logical choice was to explore what happened to Maggie in her afterlife.

Maggie was easy to write because so much of her spirit permeated the story in Haunted. It was coming up with a "bad boy" who could go toe-to-toe with her that was a challenge. Louis popped into my head with his snarky attitude and sexy-as-all-get-out Punk stylings and I ran with it. I absolutely love him and the two of them made a perfectly compelling team! I had this vision of them going on these adventures together in their afterlife intervening in the lives of the living and the afterlives of people who needed a little push before making their final choice.

While I was writing Minded, I was asked to be a part of another anthology project that would benefit Autism Awareness. The theme was New Life and I saw an immediate connection. Maggie and Louis would intervene in the lives of two new characters and help them find their way. They were perfect! The anthology ended up being postponed, but I wanted to do my part to help raise awareness for those living with Autism, so I went ahead and published Blossomed on its own. All proceeds for the months of April and May 2016 will go towards Autism Awareness.

In re-releasing Minded, I thought it would be a good idea to bridge the gap between the new stories, so I added Chapter Nine to the original story and made a few small revisions. Rereading the story fueled my desire to get busy writing Minded II, so I'm including a little snippet (proofread, but unedited) of that to keep you titillated until I can get it out to you, hopefully very soon.

So after you've read Minded and Blossomed, you might be wondering, "what's next?" I'm here to tell you that you won't want to miss my contribution to the Wicked Gods Unleashed box set coming out June 12th! In my story "The Gods of Rock 'n' Roll" you'll get a taste of the world that Maggie and Louis exist in and learn a little more about some other folks in the afterlife. Buy links are included at the end of the excerpt.

It's been a busy and sorrow-filled 2016. I have taken the loss of my rock 'n' roll heroes very hard. The deaths of Maurice White, Glen Frey, Lemmy Kilmister, and Scott Weiland were tough, but losing David Bowie and Prince was devastating. Music has been a huge influence in my life since I started dancing at age three. I remember vividly when Elvis Presley died. All of these things have weighed heavily on my mind, and influenced my writing. I included some of these folks in my stories and I created my version of the afterlife as a way to deal with my own feelings and wonderings about what happens when we die. That journey began with Maggie's story and will continue through my next several projects. I hope you will join me. Thank you for your continued support and *stay tuned for more Rock 'n' Romance!*

Love, Ro

Minded Reading Order:

Father F'in' Christmas: A Minded Prequel

Minded: A Haunted Paranormal Story

Blossomed: A Minded Story
And coming soon...
Shifted: A Magic and Mayhem Universe/Minded Book Three

BLOSSOMED EXCERPT

Blossomed: A Minded Story is one of Maggie and Louis' adventures. Come fall in love with Charlotte and Justin... And puppies!

Blossomed

On Samhain, the veil between the spirit world and the material world thins. Anything can happen, including the rebirth of those souls who weren't given the chance to blossom to their full potential. One such soul had accepted her early death as her destiny. Fate has much more in store for her.

The woman sat in the dingy gymnasium and listened with one ear to the tales of woe being shared by the others in her support group. She'd been here for an eternity, or so it seemed. It had been so long, new members rarely noticed her anymore. Some folks would try to talk to her, include her in the group, but she was more than satisfied to hear others speak. They had much more interesting things to talk about.

"Dear, you haven't shared recently. Is there anything you'd like to share?" Grandma asked her.

The woman smiled at the matron whose presence she'd come to find as comfortable as a warm blanket in front of the fire on a cold winter's night.

Comfort was difficult to find for people like her. They suffered from D.D.S., or Death Denial Syndrome. The support group was a place for them to experience an awakening, establish awareness, and ultimately, achieve acceptance of inevitable circumstances. The woman knew she was dead, had been for some time, but she didn't want to move on yet. She hadn't had much life. In death, she found relief from her pain, but the longer she listened to these people talk, the more she yearned to hear more of their experiences. It was as if she could live vicariously through their love stories and adventurous escapades. All the things she'd missed out on.

It took effort for her to speak, words leaving her at an alarming rate the less she used them. She'd forgotten her own name. Even her thoughts were vague and gray around the edges. She'd noticed in the beginning of her time here that some of the others who'd been there even longer had eventually faded away. Some fought their existence and would just blink out. Some were given other choices.

When she finally opened her mouth to speak, she realized she was now alone with Grandma.

"I'm sorry, my dear. I couldn't wait for you to find the words. It has been decided that you will be reborn. Since you haven't made a conscious choice, one has been made for you. The time is near and you will be sent on."

"But...I don't want to go back. I had a life, short as it may have been. The only reason I stayed here so long was—"

"I understand, dear. It has been decided for you. I just wanted to prepare you. You won't have an escort for the first part, so you will be on your own. Someone will meet you to help you..."

She felt a stirring in her body, one that she might have equated to a rapidly beating heart if she could recall what that felt like. Before she could protest any further, the sensation spread rapidly throughout her limbs. She began to pant and felt as though she was starving for oxygen.

"Your rebirth will be over quickly. I wish you strength and courage on your journey. It will give me great pleasure to see you find happiness."

A roaring sound filled her ears as she fought against a wave of pressure. She opened her mouth to scream just as everything went black.

Justin frowned as he strummed his guitar. No matter how many times he tried playing the chords, they just didn't sound right. It had been six months since the accident, and while he'd come much further than the doctors told him to expect, his patience with himself was running out.

He flexed his hands and winced at the lingering stiffness and pain. They were better, much better, but they just didn't want to cooperate sometimes.

He looked at the clock and saw it was time for his daily walk. Schedules and structure kept him sane, always had, but more so now that he wasn't quite at full capacity. His cognitive testing showed that some of his function had still not returned. He attended speech therapy five days a week for two hours each time and tried to relearn what had come so natural to him before. Doctors explained that where he was a year after the accident was likely where he would be for the rest of his life. That was not satisfactory for him.

"Blossom! Come. Do this."

Blossom, Justin's four year-old Great Dane, loped over to him, panting happily. She sat obediently while Justin attached her leash, her tail thumping excitedly on the rug. His girl had been a huge part of his recovery. Knowing she needed him to pull through this made it that much more important to him that he get well.

The two hopped in Justin's Range Rover and cruised across town to the San Leandro Marina. Justin was grateful he'd been cleared to drive. He preferred to walk near the water. When they arrived, he helped Blossom down from the SUV, concerned about her "delicate situation," even though his brother Jason told him not to be worried. He still wanted to clobber his brother for allowing his girl to get knocked up. Jason bred Danes with his wife as a hobby. He took care of Blossom while Justin was in the hospital and then in rehab, until he could care for her himself. He'd had a friend's stud over for a weekend to breed with his own Dane, Blossom's sister, and hadn't realized Blossom was in heat.

"It's an omen, dude. You needed a reason to get your ass movin'. I gave you several good ones! Just wait 'til you're a daddy. You're gonna love it!"

Great Dane puppies weren't exactly something Justin had planned on. His life needed to be a well-oiled machine: write, record, tour, repeat. The accident had already thrown everything off course. He just wanted things to get back to normal. He refused to accept that they never would.

It was dusk and a bit chilly as they set off, the sun setting over the Bay in pinks and lavenders. The two walked along the coastline, Justin taking care to keep his pace slow enough for Blossom and for his weary legs. He'd been fortunate to not break any bones in his limbs when he was thrown, but his head had taken a dangerous impact that had the doctors concerned. He still had issues with balance and speech...and sometimes his hands just didn't take orders. He'd been incredibly lucky on all accounts, but for an overachiever like Justin, a creative force of nature, limitations like those he was experiencing were just not something he could sit back and accept.

Speaking of sitting. Blossom had taken a seat and was staring off towards the water. Justin tried to give her a tug, but she wouldn't budge.

"Come. Make mile marker. Come on." He gave one more tug, but the one hundred thirty pound beast sat unmoved. Justin looked around to see if anyone else's dogs were acting weird, but there was no one nearby. She'd stopped about three feet from a bench, so Justin decided to take a load off, thinking maybe she just needed a breather.

"Fine," he huffed, trying to muster up some patience. He stretched his arms and legs out, feeling a bit of relief, and followed Blossom's line of sight.

The water was eerily calm. No waves broke against the rocks below the path, only faint ripples moving across the usually choppy water. Justin took a deep breath, wishing he could pick up the scent of the water, even if it was rank today, just to know that he could. Instead, he settled for the slight breeze against his face that blew his light brown hair out of his eyes.

A melody he remembered from something he was working on before the accident played through his mind and he started to sing, his voice growing in volume as he realized no one was around to hear him. The vibrations in his chest reminded him of the fact that he was alive, against all odds. He sang until he felt tears sting his eyes, letting out his frustrations. His speech might be damaged forever, but he could still sing his heart out.

Blossom lay down next to his bench after a few minutes of his singing, something she often did at home as well, and rested her chin on her front paws. She began whining softly, still staring out into the water. Justin reached down and scratched behind her ears, whispering to her that everything was okay, but her whines grew more insistent.

"Pain, girl?" Justin worried perhaps they were getting too close to her due date for her to be out walking, even though Jason assured him she had time.

"Enough today. Go Uncle Jason."

It took a few tugs to get her attention away from the water. She kept looking back as they walked to the car.

THE GODS OF ROCK 'N' ROLL EXCERPT

Meanwhile in the afterlife, things are heating up in Las Vegas. Here's an excerpt from my story "The Gods of Rock 'n' Roll."

Phillip Payne stood in the shadows and surveyed his domain. The Las Vegas branch of Neither Here Nor There was packed to the rafters on this sultry desert evening. Sweaty bodies danced in the back hall to the tunes of days past. The main ballroom was filled with the hum of conversation between guests and potential clients who remained unaware of the true nature of this destination outside the city limits. Glamour was a fabulous tool in the hands of a god like him.

Outside the night was humid. Stifling. In the summertime, even the desert air could be heavy with moisture, teasing Phillip with memories of his home and his former life in the Pacific Islands. Monsoons happened frequently, causing flash floods that could wipe out territory and end life in an instant. The weather had him feeling restless, as if something was about to shake up his little world. He just didn't know if that was a good thing or a bad thing.

He looked over the list of hopefuls invited to audition tonight and sighed. A female singer-songwriter, an alternative pretty boy looking to crossover to pop stardom, a rock band from Los Angeles, and an Elvis impersonator who was hoping to 'bring back the sound of the King.'

That one brought a curve to Phillip's full lips. It was good to be one of the King's favorites, a position he'd held for over thirty years now since the end of his mortal life. Elvis Aaron Presley, the man who became the King of Rock 'n' Roll, lived an amazing life full of adventure and accomplishment. What most people never knew was that Elvis *chose* to be born and change the face of music.

The being known as Elvis had been a quiet observer of humanity for centuries. No one really knew where he'd come from, at least none of those he'd kept close to him. They only knew that he was a powerful god gifted in many ways, particularly in music. The legend of Elvis, the man, began with the creation of the Blues. When these musicians showed up on the scene, Elvis was inspired. He decided it was time for him to be reborn and live a lifetime as a mortal human, a task all gods were required to do at some point. "Kept them honest," Elvis would say. He knew what the world needed. Rock 'n' Roll: a special blend of blues, gospel and country music, combined with a sensual swagger and sexual rebellion. His human existence changed the world. Humans began to experience music in a whole new way, and they began to actually worship the musicians who brought them joy. Once he saw this new opportunity, he cashed in on it. People thought it was the Colonel who made the decisions, but he'd been a pawn. Elvis controlled it all from the beginning. Well, except his later addiction to fried peanut butter and banana sandwiches. He never meant for that to get so out of hand.

Elvis' "death" was merely his retirement. He learned to harness this worship from humans and channel it into a way for him to straddle the line between human affairs and the afterlife. He created Neither Here Nor There as a place for both humans and the musicians who had passed, keeping the humans in the dark, of course. Those few who entered had no idea just what they were seeing, or hearing for that matter. They assumed they were just seeing a really great tribute band, something not uncommon in Las Vegas.

Being Elvis' right hand afforded Phillip a luxurious afterlife as a god of rock 'n' roll when his mortal existence came to an end. Elvis had amassed so much power from the worship of his human persona, he was able to do just about whatever the hell he wanted to, including making more gods to work for him and keep his new empire rolling in talent and the source of the gods' power: human lifeforce. Outside of the spirit, or soul, the life-force is what makes humans truly sentient and feeling beings.

As a mortal, Phillip had been blessed with the voice of an angel, albeit one that made women swoon and men envious. He also had an ear for talent and at Elvis' instruction, he fine-tuned the skills necessary to mold and shape fresh meat into superstars. Elvis made him a god and took him on as a business partner, eventually turning over his Las Vegas territory to Phillip. Along the way, other gods were created and brought in to establish branches in New York, New Orleans, and Liverpool, UK. The gods and their managers, lower immortals brought in to help run the business because of their various skills, held auditions and signed new artists to contracts. The "payment" from those contracts kept them in power, and the royalties earned by their artists added to their financial fortunes. Artists who passed on, but hadn't signed a contract, were sometimes welcomed to stay in Neither Here Nor There and play, remaining a part of the music scene forever, or they chose to end their existence and become a part of the ether. Those whose contracts ran out? Their afterlife was determined elsewhere.

People would certainly be surprised to know just how many of their favorite musicians accepted the terms and sold their souls for a career full of fame, awards, and accolade …. Or, perhaps, settled for infamy, booze, and pussy. Whatever their little hearts desired was there for the taking until time was up. Then they belonged to Phillip. He'd always been happy to collect, for with every soul he was paid, the more power he gained, and business had been *good*. These lifeforces provided the sustenance he needed to keep his little fiefdom rolling in song and cash. His afterlife was damn near perfect, or at least it had been.

Tonight, however, he felt as though everything was about to change.

It started just as so many others. The audition list displayed a few promising talents for Phillip to judge. This night in particular, three of the acts had just wrapped up the annual Warped Tour in Southern California and were scouted by one of his associates. Phillip had been pulled away from the backroom where Scott Weiland was playing a killer set with some of his House Band to listen and make decisions.

Scott was a recent arrival, and his death bothered Phillip immensely. It had been a shame that he hadn't kept it together for the entirety of his contract. His heart gave out before his lifeforce could be claimed; something that occasionally happened. Not all contracts had a definite termination date, and sometimes if interventions were unsuccessful, the artists expired before their contracts did. Scott's death was a loss for humanity, as well as Phillip's empire. But Scott had been a long-time client and friend, so when it was his time, Phillip welcomed him with open arms. The man had such a sensual vibe, a sexy-as-all-get-out delivery. His music kept Phillip feeling virile.

By the time he entered the ballroom, he was feeling antsy. On the menu first was a lovely young lady named Scarlett and her band Obsess. He took his place on his throne, which was backlit so that his face was never seen. He'd only meet the performers if they entertained him, and he thought this lass just might be entertaining.

She took the stage in her thigh high black boots and black schoolgirl skirt that flashed her panties every so often as she prowled the stage. Phillip eased back in his seat and swung a leg up over the arm, his fingers laced atop his bare abdomen. He watched with interest as the band dove right into one of their heavier numbers. Her voice had star quality. She was a decent lyricist, but not completely unique. She'd definitely be able to hold her own with any of the current crop of female-fronted rock bands. He'd give her a shot ... if she was willing to accept the terms of the contract.

He listened to two more songs before calling over Francis, one of his managers and a close friend.

"Bring her back to my office. Tell the band she'll see them tomorrow. Make sure they are taken care of with whatever or whomever they desire."

Francis smiled at him knowingly, relishing his task. Francis was completely loyal, absolutely faithful, and used discretion in all of their dealings. He'd make sure to set the band up with a night they'd never forget, so that they *would* forget.

He was mildly entertained by the preening of Salvador Kinney. He performed covers of "Carry On My Wayward Son" and "Fat-Bottomed Girls," all the while working the crowd like a pro. The kid had pipes. He had swagger. He had charisma. He annoyed the shit out of Phillip. Something was off about him. He indicated to Francis that Kinney should be passed over.

The next singer appeared on the side of the stage with her guitar and halted. Something tugged at the place where Phillip should have had a functioning heart, an organ he didn't have much need for as an immortal. Her face was hidden by the shadows, but something about her called to that miniscule bit of humanity he held deep inside. It was his only source of vulnerability that remained and not something he would ever expose to anyone ever again.

The woman appeared to be arguing with someone, and then she was gone. Just like that.

"Francis," he called out to his assistant. "What just happened?"

Francis texted Demetrius, Phillip's house manager, and received an answer quickly. "He says 'she changed her mind.' She just said, 'This is wrong.'"

"Interesting choice of words," Phillip muttered to himself. The rare human could sense the "otherness" about this place. Most were too excited about getting their big break to pay attention to their intuition. He was intrigued. She must be something special.

"Follow her. See where she goes."

"One more thing, Phillip," Francis said, looking down at his phone. "Demetrius says the kid, Kinney, has a message for you. He'll only talk to you and no one else."

Phillip smirked. "Really. Well, follow him, too. He's a loose end."

Francis sent the directions to Demetrius, who responded he would ensure it was done.

Phillip could not shake the queer feeling he'd received the moment that woman stepped on stage. It was as if she were just out of his reach. He wanted to know what it was that sent her running. But he had another woman to concern himself with for now. He made his way back to his office and took a moment to disguise himself. His natural appearance was that of a Polynesian warrior. His long, curly brown hair was pulled back tonight and he'd donned a pair of linen pants to combat the heat. But whenever he met with potential clients, he wore a suit and tamed the hair until it appeared to whomever he was meeting with that he was a clean-cut businessman. His tawny skin lightened to just barely tanned, and his piercing golden eyes darkened to a deep brown.

In either guise he was irresistible. He was fully aware of the effect he had on both men and women alike.

Scarlett was shown in and sat demurely in the chair facing his desk looking around his sparsely decorated office. His back was to her as he stood looking out over the desert. He watched her reflection in the full-length windows in front of him.

"Thank you for seeing me, Mister …?"

"You have a powerful voice, my dear. Definitely have the look. I'm impressed by the red and black dye job. You pull it off without looking cheap. Your makeup is superb. You work the stage well. Your band is mediocre, but they'll do. Your genre is growing in popularity, so you'd probably see modest success if you continue. Or … you could tone down the screaming, get a little more sensual and a little less Goth, and you might even crossover to some mainstream success. If you were to sign with me, you'd have big decisions to make about your future."

He watched her reflection as she sat quietly with stars in her eyes as he spoke. He could see her fighting a child-like grin, barely containing her excitement. Phillip turned and she instantly went from immature excitement, to womanly wantonness. It was so easy.

"The question then becomes, what are you willing to give up to see those dreams come true?"

He moved behind her chair, resting his hands on the back. She glanced up at him and blushed from her cheeks down to the swell of her breasts aching to be relieved of her push-up bra. It wouldn't take much on his part for that to happen. He just wasn't interested.

"I'd give anything to make it. I want it. I'm willing to work for it, I—"

"Anything? You should know exactly what that means before you, well, give it up."

She crossed and uncrossed her legs, then crossed them again. She pulled at her skirt. She had no game. She'd probably been able to conquer most of the men she'd encountered this far, but none of them had the weaponry he did at their disposal.

"Scarlett, you should really be careful what you wish for."

ACKNOWLEDGMENTS

Special thanks to my twinsie Marcy Cordova for helping me ready this bad boy for publication. She proofread and gave the new material a thorough onceover. I'm grateful for our chats, your feedback, and tireless support! Rock on!

To my writing partners in crime, Kimberlie and Ellay, I'm so grateful we finally got to be together in Las Vegas for the RT Booklovers Convention. It was magical! We even got to sign our first autograph as the triumvirate of awesome! Thanks also to "Ma" (aka Dorothy McAdams) for, well, sort of supervising, and for the lovely new tote. If you love custom made handbags, check out By The Sea Totes. Team Sex, Gods, and Rock 'n' Roll have plenty of good stuff in the works so STAY TUNED!

To my business pal Kelli Smith... Not a day goes by that I don't think about you and your kick-ass ways. You talk me down from my bouts of insanity and reassure me that "I got this." Thanks for helping me keep my eyes on the prize and for supporting me every step of the way!

To the super talented duo of Kerrigan Byrne and Cynthia St. Aubin... You lovely gals have inspired me and held my hand through some major periods of self-reflection lately and I am very grateful for your time and support. You both rock my world!

Thank you so much to the goddesses of the Sex, Gods, and Rock 'n' Roll Street Team! I love you all to pieces!

CONNECT WITH R.L. MERRILL

I would love to connect with you! Here's where you can find me lurking:
Facebook at: www.facebook.com/rowritesrocknromance
Email at rlmerrillauthor@gmail.com
Twitter @rlmerrillauthor
And my groovy website: www.rlmerrillauthor.com where you can find
my newsletter-y thingie and stay up-to-date with the latest from my
world of Rock 'n' Romance! You can even pick up passwords to unlock
short stories set in the Teacher, Haunted and The Rock Season worlds.

REVIEWS

Reviews are incredibly important to authors. If you enjoyed Blossomed: A Minded Story please leave your review for others at BookBub, Goodreads, or whichever rooftop you'd like to shout it from. Thank you!

www.ingramcontent.com/pod-product-compliance
Lightning Source LLC
Chambersburg PA
CBHW030607130626
46552CB00006B/2693